THE DROWNING

ALSO BY VALERIE MENDES:

Girl in the Attic
Coming of Age
Lost and Found

VALERIE
MENDES
THE DROWNING

SIMON AND SCHUSTER

SIMON AND SCHUSTER

First published in Great Britain by Simon & Schuster UK Ltd, 2005
A Viacom company

1 3 5 7 9 10 8 6 4 2

Simon & Schuster UK Ltd
Africa House
64-78 Kingsway
London WC2B 6AH

A CIP catalogue record for this book is available from the British Library

ISBN 1-416-90127-2

Typeset by SX Composing DTP, Rayleigh, Essex
Printed and bound in Great Britain by Cox & Wyman Ltd, Reading, Berks

For Captain Phil Moran
and the Royal National Lifeboat Institution, St.Ives, Cornwall,
with gratitude, admiration and love

Acknowledgements

I could not have written this novel without the help and encouragement of three people:

Captain Phil Moran, Lifeboat Operations Manager of the Royal National Lifeboat Institution, St Ives, Cornwall, who so generously shared with me his unique knowledge of both the sea and St Ives;

Liz Nolan and the students at her Theatre Dance School in Lelant, Cornwall, who put up with me practically living on the premises for a fortnight in September 2003, and who talked me through a host of technical and Cornish details;

and Angela Askew, Director and Head of Dance at The Urdang at Finsbury Town Hall. Angels not only gave me her immediate and unstinting cooperation, but also shared with me the Urdang's crucial move from their beloved banana warehouse in Covent Garden, their premises for the past thirty years, to the magnificent air and space of their new home.

"Ready, Steady, Go"

Jenna woke early that February morning.

Her room crouched in darkness.

She listened for the yearning cries of the gulls, the swirling waves of sea.

They made no answer.

Instead she heard the faint growl of Sunday traffic, pawing the streets beneath her attic room; a tube train grumbling underground; water lurching down a pipe.

Suddenly she remembered.

She was not in Cornwall.

Yesterday, on the station platform, sleet blowing across their shoulders, Dad had waved her goodbye, his eyes behind his funny round spectacles full of pride and shining with tears. She had taken the train from St Erth to Paddington. To stay with Dad's beloved sister, Aunt Tamsyn.

For a very special reason.

Jenna sat up, her heart flapping into her throat like a bird trapped in a chimney.

It had finally arrived. The first Sunday of the spring half-term.

The day that could change her life . . .

"Are you ready?"

"No," Jenna said. "How can I be? I'll never be ready, not in a hundred years."

"Nonsense." Her aunt looked Jenna squarely in the eyes. "You haven't got a hundred years, you've got half an hour to get there. You're sure you know the way?"

"Out of Goodwin's Court, turn right up St Martin's Lane . . . God, Tammy, you've shown me often enough. It's only down the road."

"And you know what they want, what they're looking for."

Jenna chanted, "Potential not perfection."

"Exactly —"

"But I haven't *done* anything. There'll be girls so much better than me. From Edinburgh, Paris, Stockholm, all over. I'm not *good* enough —"

"Oh, yes, you are. I've watched you dance, remember?

I've heard you sing and I've seen you act. I know it was only local, amateur stuff, but it was plenty good enough for me. I can spot real talent a mile off."

"But you're biased. You know it's me and you make all kinds of allowances."

"Rubbish, Jenna. Stop putting yourself down. You're better than good. You're brilliant – and you're beautiful." Her aunt's voice grew brisker. "Now, have you got everything? Pink tights, leotard, ballet shoes, jazz trousers, jazz boots, sheet music –"

Reluctantly Jenna grinned. "Arms, hands, legs, feet, head, eyes, hair, memory –"

Her aunt gave a sharp crow of laughter. "Point taken . . . Here, I've made you lunch. It's going to be a long, hard-working day. Promise me you'll eat, keep up your energy."

"Yes, Tammy." Jenna crammed the food into her bag.

"So!" Her aunt stood back and looked at her. "It's ready, steady, go, then?"

"Suppose." Jenna swung her bag over her shoulder. "I guess this is the moment." Her teeth chattered. "Eleven years of work, since I was four years old . . . all leading to this."

Stiffly, she turned towards the door, but her courage failed. She threw down her bag and leapt across the

3

narrow hallway. In her arms, Aunt Tamsyn felt like a tiny, light-boned child.

"Thanks for everything, Tammy. Your support, your encouragement —"

"*Least* I could do —"

"Being here in London, being here for me . . . Even if nothing comes of it, thanks for everything. Even if I fail."

Her aunt hugged her. Then she held her at arm's length, her eyes scanning Jenna's face, her hands gripping Jenna's.

"You won't fail, Jenna Pascoe. What have I always told you? You've got star quality."

Jenna bit her lip. "Don't know about that." She felt her aunt's confidence flowing through her, warming her veins. "But I'm going to have a bloody good shot at this. My best."

"There! You're never Elwyn's girl for nothing."

"Ready, steady, then, Tammy?"

"Go for it. I'll meet you outside the Academy at the end of the day. I'll be jumping up and down, longing to know how it went."

Jenna shot out of the door and started down the flights of narrow wooden stairs. Her feet clattered like the thunder of tap shoes on the rehearsal floor.

She heard her aunt calling after her.

"I'll be thinking of you all day, Jenna Pascoe. Just you remember that."

Jenna closed the front door behind her.

She glanced at the brass plaque, *Tamsyn Pascoe, Theatrical Agent,* ran her fingers over the lettering in a last goodbye.

Then she turned her face into the bitter wind, hunching her scarf across her throat, pulling on her gloves. Her singing teacher's voice rang in her head.

"If you are cold, you cannot sing. You must be warm, relaxed, comfortable. You sing not just with your throat but with your entire body. To look after your voice, you must attend to your health. It must become the good habit of a lifetime."

The alleyway of Goodwin's Court stood bleak and empty. A thin tabby cat with yellow eyes, prowling for food, looked up at her expectantly. He reminded Jenna of Dusty, the cat at her home in the narrow cobbled street of the Digey in St Ives. He lived in their tiny communal courtyard, belonging to them all and yet only to himself.

A wave of homesickness flooded the pit of her stomach.

Right now, Dad would be standing at the long table in their tea-room kitchen, slapping and pounding his wonderful homemade dough, singing a sea shanty happily off-key.

Her brother, Benjie, would be sitting at his desk, dissecting the insides of a radio in order to put it back together again, muttering to himself, frowning with concentration.

For a moment, Jenna longed to be with them, safe and snug in her attic bedroom opposite Benjie's; practising at the barre in the dance studio Dad had made for her above the tea room; walking through St Ives and up the steep hill of the Belyars to school, hidden among the quiet of its green fields.

Mum would be still asleep. Sunday mornings were the only ones when she wasn't up at the crack of dawn.

Jenna groaned at the thought: Mum spelled problems, big time . . .

Jenna tilted her chin in defiance. With an effort, she pushed thoughts of home aside. She walked briskly into St Martin's Lane, turned right towards Shelton Street and the old banana warehouse which for the last thirty years had been the Urdang Academy.

Towards her audition.

If she could only get it right, Tammy's flat, this short walk – and this Academy – would be her home from the autumn for the next three years. Her aunt had offered to pay the fees, to give Jenna all the support and encouragement she'd need. In spite of Mum . . .

Jenna's breath pumped into the dank, foggy Sunday-morning air. Her cheeks stung with the cold. Her heart raced with excitement.

This is it, girl.

Go for it.

And don't let anyone see just how nervous you really are . . .

The Audition

Shivering with fright, Jenna stood with nineteen other hopefuls in an awkward queue as they registered their names and were given a number and a timetable for the day. She glanced at some of them and tried to smile, but the effort was monumental. Her hands shook as she changed her clothes in silence for ballet, the first class of the day.

She pulled on her pink ballet tights and the new leotard Leah had given her. Leah, who had taught her everything she knew.

"A little present for you to kick-start the day. It's a lucky red. Most of the girls will be in black. But with your dark hair and eyes, red will look wonderful. The colour's warm and inviting – and you want to be noticed. You need to stand out from the crowd the minute you walk into the studio. Here, Jenn: wear it for me."

Jenna brushed back her long, straight hair, secured it firmly in a neat chignon. She double-checked that her ballet shoes were correctly tied; smoothed her heavy eyebrows, glossed her mouth. Hands on her hips, she took a deep breath.

Right . . . Here we go . . . I guess I'm ready as I'll ever be . . .

They zoomed into the cream-and-green-painted ground-floor studio, its upright piano perched in a corner, the pianist already behind it.

The panel of four directors sat in front of them, poised along the wall of mirrors and multiplied by them, their pens at the ready, their smiles careful, neutral, attentive.

Jenna willed herself not to look at them.

They all appear so composed and confident . . . Wish I felt like that! . . . I'm not good enough for them . . . I'm going to blow this big time . . . I'll probably fall flat on my face trying to do a pirouette and everyone will laugh . . .

Their teacher — the whisper had flown: she had once been a soloist with the Royal Ballet — introduced herself and welcomed them. She was small with grey hair cut into a spiky fringe, bright eyes and a warm, authoritative voice.

She expected them to work for a living.

She glanced at the pianist, gave him a brief nod. "Thank

you, Nick . . . Right, everyone. Shall we begin? I'd like you all to lie down on the floor . . . Use the space sensibly, please, including the corners."

First came the exercises to warm and strengthen their bodies. The routines at the barre followed, as familiar to Jenna as her own face and hands. Then the class burst into full swing. Feet in their ballet shoes pounded the floor like the drumming of horses' hooves. Jenna forgot everything else as the music and the teacher's voice took over – and as her body began to respond.

Next came the physical examination. The Academy needed to see how good their turn-out was, how flexible their feet, how strong their backs, the overall alignment of their bodies, whether they had ever had any injuries.

"Be honest," they were told. "We need to be confident that you can get through three years' work without weaknesses rearing their ugly heads. If you try to hide anything serious, you will be the ones to suffer in the end."

Jenna stood brave and tall as the steely eyes looked her over. She was lucky to have a flexible body and not to have broken any bones – but even so, she gave a sigh of relief when the inspection ended.

I felt like a fluttering moth being trapped and put under a microscope . . . Are her wings really strong enough? Do you think she can fly for ten hours at a single stretch?

The relentless pace of the day refused to slacken or give Jenna time to breathe. The Head of Dance stood in front of them.

"I'd like you to fill in these." She gave them each a blank sheet of paper. "Write me a personal statement. Tell me why you want to be here, why you want to do our course. You can tell me anything you like, as long as you really feel it and mean it."

Jenna stared down at the paper. *My dancing life in a nutshell?* She picked up her pen and began to write as fast as she could:

I went to my first dance class when I was four years old. Leah, my ballet teacher, had just arrived in St Ives and was starting up a theatre dance school. Dad said it would be a good idea if I went on Saturday mornings. My parents own and run a tea room which is open six days a week. They're always busy, so having me safe and occupied on a Saturday seemed like a good idea.

I loved it. I'd spend all week asking when I could go to Leah's again, singing the music she'd used for our class — and driving my

parents mad! Then I'd pull on my pale blue leotard, clip my frilly
skirt over it, and hop up and down, wanting to leave.

When I was six, Dad drove me up to London to stay with his
sister, my aunt, Tamsyn. She took me to see my first ballet,
Giselle, danced by the Royal Ballet. I can still remember feeling
completely overwhelmed and enchanted. I knew straight away
that that was what I wanted to do when I grew up.

Four years ago, as a special treat, my aunt took me to see
Matthew Bourne's company, Adventures in Motion Pictures: their
Swan Lake with Adam Cooper. It made me rethink everything:
the storyline, the music, the way you could dance to it.

I hope more than anything else in the world that you will take
me on. I shall work until I drop – and I promise you will not be
disappointed.

When they were asked to stop writing, Jenna gave her
piece of paper to the Head of Dance, catching in her eyes
the faintest glimpse of a smile.

After lunch – *Thanks, Tammy, I'm ravenous* – they were put
through their paces once again in a jazz class. This time
they were all in regulation black: tight tops, bell-
bottomed trousers, soft black jazz boots. And with a new
teacher: young, dynamic, with a body lithe as a snake, she

did the splits on the floor as easily and swiftly as her head-high kicks and dazzling pirouettes.

Half-way through the class, Jenna's confidence and energy began to flag. She noticed how well some of the other students were dancing, how quickly they picked up the teacher's instructions for the routine they were expected to learn on the spot.

I'm just one of the crowd. They all dance better than me. I don't know what I'm doing, apart from wasting everyone's time.

She was glad when the class came to an end.

Catching her breath, she changed back into her jeans and blue top. The rest of the afternoon passed swiftly in a haze of vocal work: group singing to warm up their voices; a solo song, followed by a monologue from a modern play she had chosen. At the end of it, Jenna's mouth felt dry. In the uncomfortable silence, her legs shook with sudden exhaustion.

"Thank you for listening," she said to the panel.

"We'll let you know your results in writing as soon as we can," the Head of Dance told her.

"I . . . I . . ." Jenna forced the words to spill out. "I hope you will want me."

Rapidly, she turned and ran: out of the studio, up the stairs, into the cloakroom. She flung on her coat, grabbed her bag, pulled off her hairband so her hair could flow long and smooth down her back.

It's over . . . it's all over . . . Now there's nothing I can do but wait . . .

Outside she realised, startled, the dark evening had already clamped its teeth.

She stood in the doorway. The black street swayed around her. A van hurtled past at hair-raising speed, its radio blaring. For a moment she could not remember which way to turn.

"Jenna?" Aunt Tamsyn emerged out of the shadows. "How did it go?"

Relief washed through Jenna's heart. "God, Tammy . . . I'm so pleased to see you."

"There now!" The birdlike hug enveloped her. "Let's go and have a celebration supper. You can talk me through every single minute of your day."

Sitting on the train going home on Monday, Jenna replayed the audition in her head. The more she thought about it, the more convinced she became that she'd failed.

Back in St Ives, Mum and Dad greeted her hurriedly, busy in the tea room. She walked through to the inner courtyard which they shared with three other cottages, and into the kitchen of their adjoining house, wondering as she did so whether she'd blown any chance of escape in the autumn.

She darted upstairs to find Benjie and tapped on his door.

"Jenn?" Benjie squinted up at her from the floor, the light glinting on his glasses. "Come and look at this."

"What on earth . . ."

An enormous plastic cage, lined with yellow straw, perched on a low table beneath the window. In one corner of the cage sat a small wooden box with cutaway windows and a door labelled TIMBER HIDEAWAY; in another a dark green plastic igloo. In the middle, a sleek furry animal with pink feet picked ferociously at a bowl of nuts and seeds.

"My new guinea pigs," Benjie said proudly. "This black-and-white one's called Klunk. The gingery-brown one, she's smaller, her name's Splat. She's asleep in the igloo."

Jenna laughed in spite of her misery. Klunk inspected her with shiny round black eyes. She knelt beside Benjie. "Where did you get them?"

"Hedley from my class gave them to me yesterday. His dad breeds them. I've wanted some for ages. They're great to watch. Klunk loves anything green: spinach, broccoli, parsley. He nibbles like crazy."

"You'll have to keep them clean as well as fed." Jenna sat back on her heels. "Aren't you going to ask me how I got on?"

Benjie stared sideways at her. "Oops, sorry, sis. I forgot. How did it go?"

"Lousy. I was total crap. I'm sure they'll turn me down."

Benjie looked startled. "Why? What happened?"

"The morning was OK, I guess, though I was shaking with nerves. But the jazz class in the afternoon was really tough. Some of the other kids were brilliant. There was one guy whose jumps were so fantastic he made me feel like an earthworm."

"Did you sing?"

"Yeah. I did that number from *Oliver!* — you know, the Artful Dodger one, 'Consider Yourself', but it came out all squeaky and my cockney accent was rubbish. One of the girls had a fantastic soprano voice which filled the whole building. It made me so depressed that by the time it came to the monologue, I nearly dried up altogether."

Benjie flung an arm round her shoulders. "I'm sure you weren't as grotty as that."

"The more I think about it, the worse I'm sure I must have done." Jenna hugged him. "Shame I couldn't sneak you in, to cheer from the back row."

Waiting

The bus swung out of St Ives and began its slow journey along the wet, late-winter road towards the villages of Carbis Bay and Lelant.

Jenna heaved a sigh of relief. Half-terms at home involved hours helping Mum and Dad in the café, or keeping an eye on Benjie. Her dance classes with Leah, which continued throughout the year, meant that most afternoons at half-past three she had a cast-iron excuse to tear off her apron and dash out of the Cockleshell Tea Room as fast as her legs could carry her.

She'd run through the narrow streets, her bag bumping against her thigh, pushing against the crowds and ducking out of the way of cars, up the hill to the coach station, longing for the moment when the bus moved through Carbis Bay into the open green fields of Lelant – and away down the right-hand bend in the road towards its village hall.

There, week in, week out, small groups of children and teenagers came and went, carrying their shoes and dance gear, filled with hopes and fears, disappointments, delights, longings and ambitious dreams.

Today would be the first time Jenna had seen Leah since her audition. She'd told her about it on the phone, but now the girls would want to hear the details. And the answer to the questions burning their way into Jenna's heart. Had she heard from the Academy? Had she been successful? Did they want her? When would she hear?

She simply didn't know. Five days had passed and still the postman had brought her nothing.

"No news is good news," Aunt Tamsyn had said to her on the phone last night — but somehow Jenna couldn't quite believe it. "There's nothing you can do but wait."

"I'm *hopeless* at waiting." Jenna stared grimly out of the living-room window at the Digey, already half-hidden in twilight, at people scurrying busily home over the cobblestones with their parcels and bags. "I'd rather do *anything* than sit around. I should be doing my coursework but I just can't concentrate."

"It won't be long now. I've met the Head of Dance several times. She's very meticulous about writing to her hopefuls as soon as she can. She knows you'll be on tenterhooks —"

"I'm that all right!"

"She has to consult the rest of the panel, they have to be absolutely sure they're making the right —"

"But they must've done that on Sunday evening, after we'd left. They were with us all day. It can't be *that* difficult to decide."

"Be patient, Jenna." Aunt Tamsyn sounded brisk and businesslike. "Don't forget, there'll be letters to write to all of you, whether you're good, bad or indifferent. And you know what the post can be like."

"Yes, but —"

"Look, if you're going to work in this business, last Sunday was just the first of many auditions. Learn to take them in your stride. You can have all the talent in the world, you know. But you also need courage and sheer dogged determination."

"I know." Jenna sighed. "Stamina and stickability —"

"Exactly. When I started my agency, I was living in a bedsit in Blackheath and I had three clients. Don't you think there were days — weeks even — when I thought I wasn't going to survive? If you crumple up and give in, fall at the first hurdle, you might as well forget the whole thing, right now."

"You *know* I can't do that —"

"So chin up, girl . . . There's someone on the other line, I've got to go . . . Ring me tomorrow."

Jenna shut her eyes. She knew exactly how her aunt looked: her face flushed from the buzz of excitement her work gave her, her long silver earrings flashing in the lamplight of her office desk. There'd be files and papers everywhere, empty coffee mugs, photographs of her clients lining the walls, all of them signed with a bold, black flourish: *To darling Tamsyn, with gratitude.*

After twenty years in the business, she'd helped so many people find fame and fortune . . . She was always so generous with her time, so loving. If only Mum could be more like that . . .

"Night, Tammy."

"Good night, Jenna. Sleep well."

She slid off the bus, breathing the air that heaved in from the sea. The land smelt of the first softening of early spring.

She pushed open the door of Lelant's village hall.

Inside, lights, voices, laughter and bustle greeted her: Leah testing the CDs were in good working order; several girls limbering up at the barre; others gossiping in a huddle; Leah's youngest daughter, Georgie, sitting on the floor in a purple leotard eating a bag of crisps.

At the end of term they were planning to give a show for charity and one of the mothers had brought in some material for the costumes. It lay in crushed piles of glittering silver and gold on the small platform.

Jenna's two best friends, Imogen and Morvah, broke from the group and came flying towards her. She'd known them both since she was four years old. In many ways, they'd grown up together, each at different schools but meeting week after week at Leah's classes. The initials of their names spelt JIM and Dad always called them the Three Jimmys . . .

Now she steeled herself for their greetings and the inevitable question: "Hi, Jenn! Have you had any news yet?"

Leah spotted the strain on Jenna's face and called a swift halt to the chatter.

"Right, girls, let's get to work . . . Exercises first, then I want to do some more choreography to the three opening routines for the show. Easter's round the corner and we've still got tons of work to do."

Jenna got through the class feeling as if her body was moving on automatic pilot. She hadn't been to Leah's class since the end of the previous week and already she felt her limbs were stiffer, less supple than they should be.

Usually I'd be completely absorbed in this . . .

Now all I can think of is how much I want to be in Covent Garden, in the Academy's ground-floor studio, the wheels of trucks and cars whizzing past the window, Nick making the piano sing like a lark.

"Jenna." Leah beckoned to her at the end of class as the other girls clambered up the stairs to the changing room. "Could I have a quick word?"

"Sure." Perspiration dripped down Jenna's back.

"Are you OK?" Leah looked anxiously into Jenna's eyes. "Are you coping?"

"With the waiting for news?" Jenna shivered slightly, her limbs rapidly losing their warmth. "Just about . . . Sorry, Leah, I danced badly tonight."

"Nobody else noticed . . . Look, I was wondering . . . Would you like to dance a solo for me in the new show?"

Jenna gasped. "I'd *love* to."

"Great. I'll choreograph a dance specially for you. Come to my studio on Sunday afternoon . . . We can start work on it then, one to one."

"Thanks, Leah." Jenna grasped her arm. "I mean, really, thank you."

"Go and get changed. Quickly, or you'll miss the bus."

Jenna turned to race up the stairs into the changing room.

"And Jenna —"

"Yes?"

"Good luck . . . Ring me the minute you have news."

Jenna stared at the front door as the letters slid through the box.

She knelt and picked up the post.

Two bills for Dad, a letter for Mum, junk mail . . .

And a letter postmarked "The Urdang Academy" for somebody called Miss J. Pascoe.

Jenna sat in the middle of the hall.

She could smell the mouth-watering scent of Dad's freshly baked bread coming from the tea-room kitchen.

She heard Mum's voice, shouting across the inner courtyard: "Where are all the clean serviettes, Elwyn? They're supposed to be in the corner cupboard."

Upstairs, Benjie rumbled his train set around his bedroom floor.

Jenna clawed at the envelope.

The notepaper shook between her fingers. The words danced in front of her eyes, upside down. She hunched her knees to her chin, held the piece of paper between finger and thumb, turned it the right way round.

Dear Jenna

I am delighted to be able to tell you that your audition on Sunday was successful . . .

Jenna screamed with joy.

She scrambled to her feet. Holding the letter as if it were her most precious possession, she started to dance around the hall, into the living room, out of the living room, into the kitchen.

She flung open the kitchen door and yelled across the communal courtyard.

"Dad! I've done it! They want me!"

He hadn't heard her. Pots and pans clattered in the tea-room kitchen, Mum's voice grumbling among them.

Jenna made a dash for the phone.

"Tammy? It's me!"

"Hi! Any news?"

"They've said yes! I can't believe it! I was so sure I'd blown the whole thing!"

"Jenna! That's fantastic! When did you hear?"

"Just now! This very minute!"

"What does the letter say?"

"I don't know, I've only read the first line!" Jenna peered at the bottom of the piece of paper shaking in her hand. "Something about them moving to new premises in the autumn . . . The Finsbury Town Hall in Islington."

Tamsyn gasped. "That's *great* news. I'd heard rumours . . . They'll have so much more space there, be able to do so much more. You can go by bus from here."

"Yes." Jenna hopped up and down. "I can't take it in . . . It's like being in a dream . Thank you so much, Tammy . . . I couldn't have done it without —"

Mum cut in abruptly. "Who are you talking to?"

Jenna turned. Mum stood in the kitchen doorway.

"Aunt Tamsyn." She breathed rapidly into the phone, "Got to go . . . Ring me tonight."

Mum frowned. "And what was *that* about?"

"I've heard from the Academy. My audition . . . I've got a place."

A look of total disbelief swept Mum's face. "*Have* you indeed!"

"Yes, I have!" Jenna said defiantly.

"I never thought you'd make it."

"You and me both . . . Well, aren't you going to say, 'Congratulations'?"

Mum smoothed her apron, trying to compose herself. "I'm not sure that's really in order. *They* may have said yes, but you need *our* approval before you go anywhere."

Jenna gasped. "There's no way I'm turning them down. Not after all that work."

"What about your GCSEs? When do you intend to take *those?*"

Jenna tried to keep her patience. "My course doesn't start until September. I'll take my GCSEs in May and June."

"I *see.*" Mum bit her lip. "But there are lots of other things to consider. Like . . ." she flailed slightly. "I'm not happy about Tamsyn's offer to pay your fees."

Jenna clenched her fists. The precious letter crumpled inside her hand. "We *agreed* that when she came to stay at Christmas, before I even applied to the Academy. We've talked about it a hundred times since then."

"You mean you and Dad have. I simply don't approve of handing you over to Tamsyn. London can be a dangerous place for young girls. I'm not at all sure I can trust her to look after you. Nothing's been finally decided."

"That's not fair, Mum. You're never interested in —"

"Oh, I'm *interested* all right." Pat, pat, went Mum's hand against her tightly permed hair. "We need you here. I want you to help me and Dad run the Cockleshell. Not rush off to London on some hare-brained scheme." She bustled across the kitchen, bent to open one of the cupboards. "Where *are* those serviettes? . . . Really, Jenna, this fairy-tale nonsense stops right now."

Jenna stared down at the redness of Mum's neck, her thick waist, the starched white cuffs of her blouse. "This 'fairy-tale nonsense'," she said, her voice deadpan, "is years of hard work. Everything I've ever wanted to do with my life."

"Prancing around on some silly little stage, pretending to be a swan." Mum stood up to look at her, her voice now openly mocking. "Come on, Jenna, get real."

Jenna unclenched the precious letter, flattened it out, waved it in Mum's face. "This *is* real . . . Leah and Tammy —"

"Filling your head with pipe dreams. It's so irresponsible of them."

"They believed in me. Now the Academy believes in me too. I've fought really hard for this and I've made it. It's out of your hands."

Mum shook her head. "We'll have to see about that."

"There's nothing *to* see . . . Except this letter. Don't you even want to read it?"

But Mum had already turned on her heel and was marching towards the door.

"Any other mother would be *pleased* for me." Jenna's voice rose, catching and then sobbing in her throat. "Dad will be over the moon."

Mum hesitated in the doorway. Without looking round she said, "Some of us have already done several hours' work today. Tell Benjie I've just made him some scrambled eggs. *He* appreciates me, even if you don't."

Jenna flung herself up the stairs.

She tapped on Benjie's door. There was the sound of wild scrabbling; a cupboard door closed. He called, "Who is it?"

"It's me."

Try not to show Benjie how Mum's upset me. Just pretend it's an ordinary day.

She pushed at the door and looked round it. "Phew! When did you last clean out that cage?"

"Last week."

"Well, do it again. Klunk and Splat are stinking this room out . . . Mum wants you downstairs."

Benjie lay on the floor, his head against a bottle-green train's engine. He looked up at her. "What for?"

"Breakfast's ready."

"Cool." Benjie hoisted himself to his feet. "Have you been crying, sis? Your face looks peculiar."

Jenna smeared a hand across her cheeks. "No, it doesn't."

"Yes, it does. It's all wet and gooey."

Jenna sniffed. "I got in."

Benjie stared, open-mouthed. "To the dance school?"

"Yes."

"And you thought you'd blown it." He bent quickly to adjust another carriage on the track. "That's brilliant, isn't it?"

Jenna bit her lip. "Yes, I suppose it is!"

"Then why do you look all peculiar?"

"I don't. Go on, Benjie. Go and eat your breakfast."

"Are you leaving now?"

Jenna gave a hiccup of laughter. "I'd *like* to leave tomorrow." She leant against the door, needing its support. "I can't go until September . . . That's when the course starts. Like any other school."

Benjie stood up. He took off his glasses and solemnly wiped them with the end of one sleeve. "So you won't live here any more."

"No," Jenna said. "I won't."

A shiver of shock flashed through Benjie's round grey eyes.

"But I'll come back in the holidays. And before you ask, you *can't* use my studio for your train set. You'll ruin the floor and I won't be able to dance on it. You're to leave the room alone, do you hear?"

Benjie hooked his glasses back over his sticking-out ears. He pushed past her, his body for a moment pressing against hers.

"Don't care about the room. It's *you*. I don't want you to go, sis. I'll have to stay here all on my own."

Slowly, Jenna followed him downstairs.

This should be the happiest day of my life. Instead it feels like the worst.

Dad came bounding across the courtyard. He swept Jenna into his arms.

"Congratulations! Brilliant girl! I knew you could do it!"

His sturdy warmth hugged around her. Tears stung persistently behind her eyes.

He held her at arm's length. "Whatever's the matter?"

"Benjie doesn't want me to go. And Mum . . ." Anger flooded through her. "She can't even be *pleased* for me. She said —"

"For goodness' sake, Jenn." Dad gripped her more tightly. "Take no notice. You *know* what she's like."

"She's dead against me going anywhere."

"She'll come round. I'll make sure of that." His hands stroked her hair, smoothed its long flow down her back. "You leave her to me."

Jenna's words were muffled against his shoulder. "Nothing's going to stop me, Dad. I swear it. Nothing and nobody."

"Course it isn't, darling. Nothing in the world can stop you now."

Playing with Friends

As spring tiptoed across Cornwall, Jenna flung herself with renewed enthusiasm and vigour into a complex maze of work that left little time for anything — or anyone — else.

After school, she had her numbers in the new show to rehearse, her solo to learn and make perfect, costumes to be made for her and fitted, her regular ballet, tap, contemporary dance and theatre classes to keep her fit and supple.

Her private singing lessons continued with her teacher, Helen, as they extended Jenna's range of songs.

"Lift the notes off the page with your energy. Let me hear the brightness . . . Out of it comes interpretation . . ."

Helen sat at the piano in her elegant living room, her hands skimming the keys. Jenna felt the blood rising in her cheeks, her lungs filling with air.

"Good . . . Excellent . . . Smile and let me see those cheekbones changing the shape of your face and the sound of the notes."

In early April, Jenna's sixteenth birthday came and went without much time for celebration. After the success of the Easter show and its standing ovations for her solo on each of the three performance nights, the local paper published a feature about her, with a large photograph. People in the street recognised her and called out their congratulations. Neighbours came to the tea room to tell Mum and Dad how much they had enjoyed the show.

Dad said he was delighted.

Mum gave them a fleeting smile but made no comment.

"When September comes," Dad told Jenna one Sunday afternoon as they walked on their own along the cliff path towards Zennor, "when your term begins, Mum'll be fine, you'll see. I've persuaded her that Tamsyn will look after you."

"Of course she will," Jenna said.

"I'll keep Mum busy with new autumn menus to test and serve. She'll have plenty of other things on her mind. Her bark is worse than her bite. I reckon she's just finding it hard to let you go. And maybe she's a bit jealous. I think she misses London life herself."

A showery wind flapped into their faces, tugged playfully at Jenna's hair. Far below, massive grey swells of sea heaved into dark coves like hungry lions searching for their prey.

"I'm dreading the scene she'll make," Jenna said.

"We'll get you packed and organised and on that train before she can say raspberry jam. Benjie will be eleven in June, he'll be off to St Ives School in the autumn, just like you were. She'll have him to love and care for. And she'll have me and Tamsyn to battle with if she goes on making a fuss."

"Thanks, Dad." Jenna gripped his hand more tightly.

"You've worked for it, Jenn. You deserve to move on."

"I'll miss you when I leave."

The wind grabbed her words, whipping them around her head and out to the sea.

"And *I'll* miss *you*." Dad turned to look at her. "More than you'll ever know."

Jenna had to revise for eight GCSEs.

Formal classes came to an end in the middle of May, but she climbed the steep hill of the Belyars back to school during the rest of May and the first half of June for each separate exam.

Hang on in there, she told herself repeatedly through gritted teeth.

I'm beginning to feel like an exam machine, a robot stuffed with information. Press a button and any fact you like will come spilling out. I just hope it's the right fact!

I can't wait for history. That'll be the last exam. Reckon I haven't done too badly in the others. I've been organised and thorough. Nothing brilliant, but at least I've given them what they want!

The moment GCSEs were over, Jenna began working full-time on her ballet.

Every morning began with a practice session in her own studio. Every day she had a class with Leah. Every evening she would be back in her studio again, at the barre, repeating the day's class, finding tiny sections of it that needed further work.

In the middle of July, Jenna would take her Advanced One ballet exam and Leah was hoping that she would pass with Honours. Three other students were preparing for the same exam, and although the Academy had accepted Jenna no matter what the result, working for the exam became increasingly important to her as the summer progressed. For an hour and a half, she would dance solo for a senior examiner from the International Dance Teachers' Association.

As she caught an early bus to Lelant that morning, the air fresh and cool before the heatwave took proper hold, Jenna felt the familiar tingle of excitement pulling at her heart.

One more challenge before I'm off the hook . . .

This afternoon, Imogen, Morvah and I are going for a swim on Porthmeor Beach.

And tonight one of Morvah's friends is giving a party. His name's Denzil or something. That'll probably end up on the beach too.

Welcome to the world of the living . . .

She pushed at the door of the village hall.

The laughter, chaos and bustle of a normal class day had vanished. Everything felt quiet and serious as, under the beady and demanding eyes of the examiner, the students were put through their paces, one by one.

Jenna changed into her dance clothes. She pulled on the lucky red leotard Leah had given her for the Academy audition. Jenna had washed it and kept it hidden in a drawer until this very moment.

Carefully she tied on her soft-pointe shoes, going through the order of the exam in her head. First there would be barre work – careful, exact, meticulous and graceful. Next she'd walk into the centre of the hall for movement of the arms and centre practice. Slow movements and light, springy movements would follow; then *enchaînement,* movements linked like a chain that the examiner would give her and expect her to learn on the spot. Finally, with her full-pointe shoes, she'd dance the set, formally choreographed ballet variations.

She tied back her hair, breathing deeply, summoning her energy and every skill she had ever learnt.

Once more into the fray . . .

Go, girl, go . . .

When it was over she felt sweaty and light-headed.

The hall pumped with heat and tension. Jenna changed back into her jeans and T-shirt, hugged Leah, waved to her from the door and closed it behind her.

She'd know the results of the exam in August.

Until then, she intended to squeeze every single drop of happiness out of every moment of freedom.

Mum brushed crumbs from the lunch table into her hand. Beads of perspiration hung on her chin and slithered down her neck.

"This heat is killing me." She glanced at Jenna. "Are you going to Porthmeor Beach?"

"Yes." Jenna stood up. "I'm meeting –"

"Take Benjie with you, please. I can't have him under my feet all afternoon and it's much too hot and stuffy for him upstairs. He was off sick from school for the whole of the week before last, and I hardly had a minute to look after him."

"But Mum –"

"Don't argue with me. I've been up since five o'clock. We've been run off our feet since the minute we opened the door. Kindly pull your weight when I ask you to."

"I don't want to go," Benjie said quietly. "I'm perfectly all right in my room with Klunk and Splat."

"You've been up there all morning, sweetheart, it's not good for you. Go and change into your swimming trunks." Mum glared at Jenna. "Just keep an eye on him, would you? If that's not *too* much to ask."

"OK, if you insist," Jenna said irritably, Mum's bad temper beginning to rub off on her. "Stop making such a fuss."

"By the way," Mum was still glaring at her. "When I went to pay the milkman this morning, there was some money missing from my purse."

"Well, don't look at me," Jenna said furiously.

Benjie scraped his chair back from the table and vanished upstairs.

"Oh?" Mum raised her eyebrows. "So who else took it, I'd like to know?"

"I had *nothing* to do with it. I wouldn't go *near* your –"

Mum shrugged. "I can't be bothered to argue," she said. "I really can't."

"Come on then, Benjamin Pascoe." Jenna smiled at him. "What have you got there?"

"My book of crossword puzzles." Benjie wore his dark blue swimming trunks and a floppy blue-and-white-striped T-shirt. "Can't we do something else? I don't *want* to go to the beach."

They stood together in the doorway of the Cockleshell. Crowds swarmed down the Digey towards the beach, carrying surfboards and swimming gear, pushing impatiently past each other.

"Why? What's wrong?"

He stared down at his toes, wiggling them in his open sandals. "It's too hot and noisy . . . There are too many people . . . Really big kids . . . They scare me."

"Don't be daft, Benjie. There's nothing to be frightened of. The sea will be calm and flat as anything. You can have a great swim, splash about, cool off in the water."

He muttered, "Don't *like* swimming."

"Why not?"

He looked up at her. "Because I have to take my glasses off and then I can't see anything."

Startled, Jenna said, "Surely you can see *something*."

His round grey eyes stared into hers. "Not a lot . . . not enough."

"Has your sight got worse?"

He hesitated. "Don't know . . . Maybe . . . A bit . . ."

"Have you told Mum?"

"No. She'll go ballistic."

"Benjie, if your sight's getting worse, you must *tell* someone. Otherwise —"

"If I don't keep my glasses on, I could get lost."

Jenna gave him a hug. "We'll stick together on the beach. You don't have to swim if you don't want to."

"Mum said I did."

"Well, she's not going to know, is she?" Jenna's patience started to evaporate in the heat. "Look, Benjie, don't make a song and dance about it. I'll swim too. We'll put your glasses somewhere nice and safe, and I'll come into the water with you."

He clutched her hand more tightly. "Promise?"

"I promise. I won't let you out of my sight." She ruffled his hair. "Come on, Benjie. Imogen and Morvah will be wondering where I am."

Jenna and Benjie stood for a moment looking out over the great arc of Porthmeor Beach: to their left, the sweep of headland called Man's Head; to their right, the enormous craggy promontory of the Island, the deep rock pools beneath it.

Jenna spotted Imogen and Morvah. They had commandeered a right-hand corner of the beach where a clutch of dark rocks provided shelter, a smidgen of privacy, and space to gossip without being overheard.

Jenna pulled Benjie through the crowds towards them.

"Hi, Jenn! Thought you weren't coming . . . Why is Benjie with you? . . . Here, Jenn, sit here . . . How did the exam go? You *are* a glutton for punishment . . . Are you coming to Denzil's party tonight?"

Jenna settled herself beside them. Benjie sat down on the sand a little way apart and quickly immersed himself in a crossword puzzle. Jenna described the details of the exam, her relief now that the work was over. Then she spread herself on her towel and looked about her.

The beach was thick with bodies in various stages of undress.

"There must be five thousand people here . . . and at least five hundred in the sea."

"Are you going to swim?" Imogen asked.

"In a while," Jenna said slowly. She turned on to her stomach, spread out her arms. The heat of early afternoon had scorched the sand beneath her fingers. "I'll go for a swim with Benjie in a while."

The sounds of Porthmeor drifted into her ears: shrieks of delight from the swimmers, the splash of surfboards, a plane purring overhead, laughter from a group nearby, a mother scolding her child, the soft thud of feet pulling their way through mounds of dry sand.

She felt tired . . . so tired . . . All that work, all those exams were over . . . Now she could let herself relax . . . flop . . . even sleep . . .

She closed her eyes . . .

She dreamt she was in a terrible hurry to catch the train to London at St Erth. She just caught it as it pulled out of the station.

The baking-hot carriage was entirely empty, but she could not decide where to sit. Suddenly the carriage became the ground-floor studio at the Academy. The Head of Dance stood in the middle of the room, wearing a scarlet bikini.

She read out a list of names, but Jenna's was not among them.

Jenna cried, "But you've forgotten me, you haven't said my name . . ."

People on the beach were shouting.

Jenna woke with a start, her shoulders burning.

She sat up.

"Where . . . What's the matter? What's happened?"

"It's OK." Morvah put down her novel. "I've just been to find out. There was an accident off Man's Head. Some guy was messing about on his own on a Lilo. He fell into the sea. Luckily, someone spotted him from the cliff path and raised the alarm."

"Will he be OK?"

"The lifeguards are on to it." Imogen rooted in her bag for a comb, started to tug it through her blonde curls. "They do an amazing job."

Jenna touched her shoulders and winced. "I forgot to put on any suntan lotion."

She looked across at the spot where she had last seen her brother. The book of crossword puzzles lay on its side. Sand around it had been trodden over several times.

"Where's Benjie?"

Imogen said, "He's playing with some friends."

"What friends?"

"I don't know, do I? Three or four of them came up to him, asked him to go and play. They're over there, on the rocks, paddling around in the pools."

"But I promised —"

"Don't worry about him, Jenn. He'll be OK. We can have more of a juicy chat without him."

"Sure." Jenna stood up fast.

Too fast.

The beach swayed slightly.

"Course he'll be OK . . . Think I'll just go and check."

Jenna thrust her feet into her flip-flops, tied her towel around her waist and pushed her way through the clusters of bodies towards the rocks and their pools.

A group of children, none of whom she recognised, raced towards her, holding small bottles full of murky water.

They vanished into the crowd.

She began to pick her way over the rocks.

Benjie must be with the guys he went off with, just around the corner.

A man and a young boy fished for crabs, their trousers turned up to their knees. A woman swimmer lay panting on a boulder, her hair dripping, catching her breath for the next underwater venture. Above the rocks, sitting on a bench reading a newspaper, a silver-haired gentleman took the air and enjoyed a peaceful afternoon.

At Jenna's feet, the sea devoured the edges of the rocks as the tide rose and the swell increased.

She called, "Benjie? Where are you?"

She stumbled on a limpet-covered rock. It badly grazed her heel. She swore under her breath.

"Benjie? Come back at once. Do you hear me? This minute. Come back to the beach, where I can keep an eye on you."

A wave grumbled against the rocks. Spray showered Jenna's burning shoulders, making her gasp. She struggled on, round the vast corner of craggy boulders, further and then further still.

The sea and the rocks played smilingly with each other, empty of humankind. Above them, the sky basked, endless, cloudless, impersonal.

Jenna shrieked Benjie's name into the blue.

The murmurs of the sea thrummed into her ears.

No answer came.

Hurriedly, she slithered back over the rocks to the beach.

"Did you find him?" Imogen asked.

Morvah said, "Put your shirt back on. Your shoulders are bright red. And your heel's bleeding. You need to —"

"What I need is to find Benjie!" Jenna snapped. "Could you help me search the beach? He can't just have vanished into thin air."

"What Have I Done?"

One of the lifeguards sat on his rescue buggy by the edge of the sea.

Jenna tugged at his shoulder. "I need your help. My little brother's gone missing."

He turned swiftly towards her. "When did you last see him?"

"My friends saw him about two hours ago, over by the Island."

"Where have you looked?"

"All over the beach. Imogen and Morvah and I, we've asked hundreds of people. Nobody's seen him. He should have stayed with me, but I fell asleep. I think he may have gone off to the rock pools with some friends."

"Ah . . . Those pools can be very tricky. We can't see them all from here."

Jenna could taste sand in her mouth, feel its grit in

her eyes and under her fingernails. "We can't find him anywhere."

The lifeguard spoke clearly and concisely into his two-way radio. Then he looked at Jenna. "My colleague at the Lifeguard Hut will put out a call for him through our megaphone."

"Thank you."

"Middle of July, height of the season . . . Happens all the time on a beach as crowded as this. I'm sure he'll turn up . . ." He looked at her more closely. "What's his name?"

Jenna's cheeks and shoulders burnt, while her stomach clutched cold as ice.

"Benjamin Pascoe. Everyone calls him Benjie . . . Please, could you hurry . . . I'm really worried that something may have happened to him. My friends are still searching the beach, but if he was here we should have found him by now."

"Climb on the buggy. I'll run you back to the Lifeguard Hut and we can take it from there . . . You'll need to give us a full description . . . How old your brother is, the colour of his hair, what he's wearing. All the details you can."

Calling Benjie Pascoe . . . Has anyone seen Benjie Pascoe? If there's a Benjie Pascoe on the beach, would he please go

immediately to the Lifeguard Hut at the top of the beach . . .
Calling Benjie Pascoe . . . He's eleven years old with fair hair and
glasses . . . He's wearing blue swimming trunks and a blue-and-
white-striped T-shirt . . . If Benjie Pascoe is on the beach, please
come at once to the Lifeguard Hut where your sister, Jenna, is
waiting.

The second lifeguard's confident husky voice made the crowds sit up and listen.

"Thank you," Jenna muttered. Her teeth chattered with dread. She scanned the beach yet again, praying for the sight of Benjie's fair hair, his sticking-out ears, his glasses, his T-shirt.

"How long do we wait before we . . . before you –"

"Couple of minutes. Usually they turn up pretty quickly."

"And if they don't?"

The lifeguards glanced at each other.

The second one said, "I think we'll alert Falmouth Coastguard . . . We've just done that for the guy off Man's Head . . . Luckily, we managed to rescue him in time . . ."

"What'll the coastguard do?" Jenna asked, trying desperately to make her voice sound calm. The lifeguard's dark brown eyes were full of sympathy.

"Ask the RNLI to relaunch the inshore lifeboat . . . and then to back it up with the offshore Mersey lifeboat."

"The big lifeboat?" Her heart lurched. "You'll bring the big one in? The one where you set off the maroons?"

"That's right."

Jenna closed her eyes. How often, lying on her narrow bed in the attic room opposite Benjie's, had she heard the two dreadful thunders of the maroons, the finality of their boom; felt the way they made her heart beat and her room shake with the sound? How often had she thought, *Please God, whoever it's for, keep them safe.*

Now St Ives would hear that sound again – only this time it would be a cry of help, a warning of danger, a call for her own brother.

The second lifeguard patted her shoulder reassuringly. His hand felt cool against her burning skin. "Don't panic. I'm sure your brother's wandered off with some of his mates. Nine out of ten cases turn up again and no harm done."

Jenna said through icy lips, "And what if Benjie's number ten?"

"We'll do everything we can," the lifeguard said briskly, doing his level best to keep up Jenna's spirits. "Don't forget we've also got air-sea rescue capacity. A helicopter can be with us from Helston in eight minutes."

"I must go and tell my parents." Jenna shook with terror at the thought of what they would say to her. "They own the Cockleshell Tea Room."

"We'd prefer you not to leave the scene. You're what we call our first informant. Could you get one of your friends to go?"

Jenna spotted Imogen and Morvah walking despondently up the beach towards her.

"Yes," she said. "I'm sure they'll go for me."

As Jenna waited, the sound of the maroons rang through the streets, once and then again. People had gathered along the road above Porthmeor Beach, staring, pointing, gossiping.

Mum and Dad, with Imogen and Morvah behind them, fought their way through the crowds.

Dad clasped Jenna in his arms.

They stood and watched.

They stood and waited.

There was nothing they could do but watch and wait.

And pray.

I don't know what's happened to you, Benjie, but please, please come back to us. Just turn up on the beach, or come marching through the door of the Cockleshell with some silly excuse. Any excuse will do . . .

I should have looked after you. I shouldn't have fallen asleep. I didn't mean to. I was going to take you for a swim.

We'll do that tomorrow. After you've come back and you've had your tea and a good night's sleep, we'll come down here in the morning and we'll go for a swim.

The small inshore lifeboat circled the rocks off the Island.

The offshore Mersey lifeboat roared in to give it back-up.

High overhead, the rescue helicopter zoomed into the sky.

Jenna said through icy lips, "That was quick."

She screwed up her eyes. She could see the helicopter's whirring rotor blades as it searched the immediate area; heard its patient, insistent drone.

Suddenly it hovered in one position. A diver slid like a snake down the wire and into the water. The inshore lifeboat closed in.

The crowd fell silent.

Somewhere in the distance a voice shouted, "They've found him!"

The diver emerged with a limp body. The inshore-lifeboat crew helped him lift it into the lifeboat. After a few moments, the diver, carefully holding the body, was winched up into the helicopter.

Jenna turned her head away.

I can't look any more . . . I can't bear to look.

She hid her face on Dad's shoulder. He gripped her waist.

"Hold on, Jenn . . . It's going to be all right."

The second lifeguard stood awkwardly in front of them, his arms hugging his bronzed body.

"They'll take Benjie to Truro Hospital," he said slowly. "They'll do everything they possibly can for him."

Her face chalk-white, her lips a purple-grey, Mum said, "Get me to Truro, Elwyn. Now. Quickly. As fast as you can."

Dad said, "Of course, dear . . . Anything you —"

"Benjie isn't dead, Elwyn. The minute he sees me . . . He's going to be just fine, you'll see." Her eyes glittered, black as polished coal. "Now, as fast as you can."

Jenna began to hurry with them back along the Digey. Mum elbowed her out of the way.

"*She,*" she hissed at Dad as he took her arm, "can stay behind . . . I don't want her beside me, I don't want her in the car or at the hospital. Just get her out of my sight."

Jenna opened her mouth to plead with Mum, but no words came.

She dropped behind on the narrow street, the crowds threatening to swallow her. She could hear Dad saying, "Come *on,* Lydia. Benjie will want us *all* to be with him . . . Jenna never meant this to happen."

Mum pulled her arm out of his and marched ahead of him.

They reached the tea room.

Dad swung round to Jenna, his eyes pleading. "Do you mind, Jenn?"

Her fury with Dad bubbled to the surface. "Of *course* I mind! I'm *desperate* to see Benjie!"

Dad shook his head, took her hands, pressed the keys into them. "We'll be back as soon as we can."

She watched helplessly as Dad opened the car door for Mum; climbed into the driving seat; hurtled the car into reverse, its horn blaring; drove out of the Digey and away.

The keys throbbed in her fist. The three tables outside the front of the Cockleshell were littered with dirty cups and plates. On one of them sat a small pile of coins. Jenna stared down at them, wondering confusedly why the money had not been taken or the tables cleared.

Imogen and Morvah came racing up to her.

"Is there anything we can do?"

Imogen's face was streaked with tears. Morvah looked exhausted.

Jenna stood huddled in their arms for a moment, willing herself not to cry.

"No, I'll be fine. I'll ring you."

She released her friends, steeling herself for whatever lay ahead.

"I need to be on my own."

"Are you sure? We could help. Just tell us what —"

Speechless, Jenna turned away.

Imogen called, "Ring me. Any time. Promise me, Jenn. The minute you have news."

Jenna unlocked the tea-room door and closed it against the sun.

The room baked in the afternoon heat. A fly buzzed angrily above one of the tables, then settled itself noisily in a pot of cream.

She walked stiffly into the kitchen. The sweet scent of pastry filled the air, making her feel sick.

She threw open the door to the inner courtyard.

Dusty crouched in a shady corner, his yellow eyes circling the erratic flutters of a butterfly.

Jenna scooped the cat into her arms. She held his slender body against her face, smoothing the fur between his ears, murmuring into them.

"Benjie didn't want to go. He told me. He said it scared him — the noise, the beach, the crowds. I didn't listen, did I? I promised I'd look after him."

Jenna's legs gave way beneath her.

"Oh, my God, Dusty. What have I done?"

Aftermath

Jenna lay curled up in a ball in the middle of her studio floor.

As if she were in a trance, she'd fed Dusty, cleared the tea room of its half-eaten meals, piled the dishes into the dishwasher, tidied the kitchen, bundled a tray of freshly baked jam tarts into the freezer. She'd polished the tables, swept the floor, emptied the tiny vases of daisies, counted the money in the till, bagged it up and stacked it in the safe.

Sweat dripped down her back. Her grazed heel smarted, her shoulders burnt.

She'd picked up the phone and asked for the number of Truro Hospital. The pencil broke as she scribbled it down. It didn't matter. She knew she'd never find the courage to dial it.

Upstairs, she'd stood for a long time in the doorway to

Benjie's bedroom, watching Klunk and Splat scuttle around their cage.

She'd taken a shower and washed her hair, put on cotton pyjamas, made a cup of tea, waited until it was stone cold before she swilled it down.

The sickness at the bottom of her stomach subsided into a dull ache.

She felt numb.

When the phone rang she leapt to answer it.

"Dad?"

"I'm so sorry, Jenn." His voice choked. "They did everything they could. The helicopter crew, the staff at the hospital. They've all been marvellous. Benjie had –" His voice petered out.

"Dad, talk to me . . ."

"It looks as if he'd got himself caught . . . trapped under one of the rocks . . . There was nothing they could do for him. It was just too late."

She hauled herself upstairs to her studio and shut the door.

The slow twilight had begun. Through the window she could see gaggles of tourists, strolling, laughing, out for their evening meal; couples with their arms around each other, kissing in doorways; gangs of teenagers carrying cans of beer, jostling their way down to celebrations on the Saturday-night beach.

I'd forgotten . . . It's Denzil's party . . . I said I'd ring Imogen . . .

I should ring Tammy . . .

I can't . . . I can't do anything . . .

If I lie on the floor, I'll still be able to hear Dad's car when they get back.

She must have fallen asleep.

The studio door opened.

"Jenn? . . . Are you all right?"

Dad bent over her.

She blinked at the light shining from the landing behind him.

She sat up. "I've been waiting for you."

He knelt beside her, took her hands in his. "Mum's gone straight to bed."

Her voice hoarse and rasping, Jenna said, "How could you leave me here, all on my own?"

"I'm sorry, Jenn." Dad hung his head. "You know what Mum's like when —"

"You're *scared* of her." She pulled her hands away. "You *never* have the guts to stand up to her, no matter what she does." Desperately, she forced the words out of her dry mouth. "Now I'll never see Benjie again."

"Why are we fighting?" Dad's mouth trembled. "We shouldn't be. Not now. Not over this . . . Please, Jenn . . . I haven't got the strength."

Jenna looked at him. She'd never seen such misery in his eyes. She held out her arms.

They clung to each other although no tears came.

Jenna lay sleepless on her bed, on top of it, in her pyjamas.

It was too hot even for a sheet.

She stared at a sliver of moon which shone, still and quiet, in its inky sky. Its thin, clear light filtered through her attic window, floating the room in blue-black shadows.

Round and round in her head, in hideous repetitive swirls, spun the same questions.

What had happened to Benjie?

Who had he gone off with?

Why had he gone so far round the craggy boulders of the Island? Cold, often surprisingly deep, their pools were hard to wade in. Once he'd turned the corner, he must have known he could not be seen by people on the beach, nor could he see them.

Was he on his own by that time, and if so why?

If he'd got into trouble, why hadn't he shouted for help? If he'd been with friends, why hadn't *they* fetched someone when they saw there was a problem?

And then the final question, the one that refused to let Jenna's eyelids close.

Why had she broken her promise to Benjie not to let him out of her sight?

As the moon's light faded and dawn broke, Jenna sat up. She felt aching and cold, her heart hardening to the tasks she had to do, that had to be done.

Stiffly, she climbed into jeans and a cotton sweater, scraped her hair into a ponytail. As she crossed the landing, she heard rustling coming from Benjie's room. Shivers of surprise and dread leapt down her spine. She pushed at the door.

Klunk had somehow managed to escape. He was on the bed, beavering his way across a pillow, weird, lumpy, like a large black-and-white mouse, looking for food – maybe looking for Benjie himself.

Jenna flushed. After several vain attempts she managed to catch him in the palms of her hands, felt his tiny feet scrabbling against her skin. She put him back in his cage, watched as Splat emerged from the igloo to greet him.

I forgot to feed them last night. They must be starving.

She picked up the cage and carried it downstairs to the inner courtyard.

It's cooler down here. Benjie kept their food in a special cupboard in the kitchen. I'll remember to feed them. I'll be able to keep an eye on them, say hello to them every now and again . . . Poor little things.

Dusty sniffed at the bars and mewed against her legs.

She bent to pick him up.

"Mouths to feed," she murmured into his fur. "But not Benjie's. Not ever again."

"Mum's still in bed," Dad said an hour later. "The hospital doctor gave her a sedative. It's knocked her out."

He stood in the middle of the tea-room kitchen, looking bewildered.

"Thought I'd bake some special walnut bread . . . Where did I put the flour?" His voice broke. "Can't remember . . . Can't seem to get my act together."

"I've stuck a piece of paper on the tea-room door," Jenna said firmly. "It says, 'Sorry, we're closed until further notice.'"

Dad said wildly, "You can't do that."

"I just have."

"We'll lose all our customers."

"No, we won't. The tourists can find somewhere else to eat for a couple of weeks. St Ives is crawling with cafés. Our regulars will have heard what's happened. They'll understand – and they'll be back. Nobody could expect us to open tomorrow as if nothing –"

"But the money!"

"This isn't about money, Dad. We'll manage."

"So when –"

"When you're *ready*." Jenna perched on a corner stool. "We've got stuff to do."

"You mean –" Dad's face sagged – "Benjie's funeral."

"Yes. There'll have to be an inquest . . . and a funeral. And last night, I was thinking. Benjie's school –"

"What about it?"

"The Head. She'll need to know what's happened. She'll want to make an announcement about him. She has to be told."

Dad peeled off his glasses. He wiped his face with his sleeve. "Does she?"

"I thought I'd go to see her, at her house, this afternoon. Leah will be able to tell me where she lives. Benjie went off with guys he knew. I want her to ask his class whether anyone was with him yesterday, whether any of them knows what happened." Jenna's head started to throb with the persistence of her thoughts. "I expect the police will go to the school, talk to Benjie's class, maybe to the *whole* school. I don't know."

"I can't handle this." Dad shook on his feet.

"Yes, you can." Gently, Jenna took his glasses out of his hand. She polished the lenses with a clean paper serviette. "Here. Go and sit down. I'll make a pot of coffee. Then we'll write a list."

"What kind of –"

"Everything we need to do, the people we need to ring, the order in which everything's got to be done and who's going to do it." She dug a piece of paper out of her pocket. "Here . . . All our suppliers. You'll need to tell them as soon as possible we don't want deliveries this week. Otherwise we'll have crates of vegetables and cheese and ham sitting in the courtyard at dawn."

Dad slumped at one of the tea-room tables. "We've got to get through this, haven't we?" He put his head in his hands.

"Yes," said Jenna firmly. "We have."

Dad raised his head. "Jenn."

"What?"

"This list . . . Could we leave Mum off it?"

"What do you mean?"

"She and Benjie . . . you know . . . he was the light of her life."

"You don't need to tell *me* that!"

"I don't know how she's going to cope without him. Last night in the car, she said some terrible things. If we could take the chores off her back for a bit, do them ourselves, just the two of us, I think she'll —"

"Fine," Jenna said bitterly. "We'll leave Mum off the list."

"We can tell her about all the arrangements, can't we? You know, for the funeral and everything. Pretend we're consulting her. Just so she knows what's happening."

"Sure. Whatever."

"Jenn?"

She paused with her hand on the coffee grinder.

Dad said, "Don't know what I'd do without you."

Jenna pressed the button. The grinder screamed into life.

Without me, you'd still have a son.

That's what Mum is lying upstairs thinking . . .

Blaming it all on me.

There isn't a chance in hell now that we'll ever make it up.

*

Afterwards, Jenna had no clear memory of how she survived the next two weeks.

She only knew she had to be strong: for herself, for Dad, for those she loved and who had loved Benjie. Aunt Tamsyn, trapped at an agents' casting conference in New York, in tears on the phone, could not be at the funeral. Everybody else was there: the Head from Benjie's school, Leah, some of her older students who knew Jenna, some of Jenna's schoolfriends, Imogen and Morvah, standing either side of her, Dad and what looked like half of St Ives, regulars at the tea room, friends he had known since childhood.

They stood in the churchyard in Carbis Bay, under a relentless beating midday sun, watching helplessly as Benjie's coffin dropped into the baked earth.

Mum gave a shout of pain.

The morning they reopened the tea room, Mum came downstairs in her bathrobe. She passed Jenna on the stairs, gestured with her head to follow. Her face gleamed pearly white, her hair beneath its black tint pushed grey as a badger.

She stood in the tea-room kitchen, watching her husband as he sliced fresh vegetables for the summer salads.

"I'm not doing this any more," she said.

Dad turned to look at her.

"Lydia, dear! I'm so pleased you're up and about."

"I said I'm not doing this any more."

"What do you mean?"

"*She* can take over."

"Who?"

"*Her.* This daughter of yours. She knows why."

Dad put down his knife. Its stainless steel glinted on the chopping board, lying among the gleaming tomatoes and crisp radishes like a dead fish.

"But, dear, she'll only *be* here for another few weeks. Next month, she's off to London, to —"

"Oh, no, she isn't."

Jenna's heart locked into her body, a frozen lump of ice.

"If you think she's going anywhere after this, Elwyn, you're very much mistaken. She can stay here and *work* for a living."

Jenna took a few steps into the kitchen. "I've *been* working for a living . . . These last few months, I've never worked harder in my life. Don't you understand? That's why I fell asleep on the beach. I was —"

Mum rounded on her, her eyes blazing with fury. "Excuses, excuses. Always got them, haven't you? With your fancy airs and graces, pirouetting through life like a fairy on a Christmas tree."

Dad said, "*Please,* Lydia, leave the girl alone."

Mum turned to him. "I'm going upstairs for a long hot bath. Then I'm off to the hairdresser. Then I shall take myself out to lunch and to the cinema. Then I'll have a cup of tea on the harbour, do a spot of shopping, whatever takes my fancy. OK?"

Dad looked across at Jenna, his eyes behind his glasses flat and dull.

He said, "Yes, dear . . . Have a good day."

They closed the tea room and cleared up. Dad cooked a light supper that neither of them wanted. Jenna turned on the television, aware that Dad was pacing up and down, clicking his fingers and humming, hovering by the door, staring anxiously out of the windows.

When the clock struck nine, he said, "Reckon I should . . . you know . . . go for a little walk, meet Mum coming back, just in case she —"

Jenna flicked off the television. "Want me to come with you?" she asked casually.

"Sure," Dad said. "Thanks, Jenn. Nice evening for a stroll."

Trying to pretend nothing was wrong, they marched swiftly up the Digey and into Fore Street. Grumbles of thunder threatened in the distance. The first few drops of warm rain plopped on to the cobblestones.

"I'll start looking in the shops from the harbour end," Dad said. "You start at the top and work down."

They met in the middle.

"Nothing," Jenna puffed. "The bookshop's closed, of course, so are all the clothes shops. Tried the art gallery, the deli, the fish-and-chip place."

"I've checked everywhere," Dad said. "No sign."

"You know that little shop at the bottom of St Andrews Street? The one that sells magic stuff, stones and shells and beads? It stays open late. Maybe —"

Dad shook his head. "Mum calls it mumbo jumbo, you know she does." His face brightened. "Got it! She'll be having a cup of tea on the harbour. That's where she said she'd —"

"Dad," Jenna said patiently. "It's half-past nine."

They started to run: down to the harbour, checking every other shop and restaurant between them.

Jenna burst into the Café Pasta, glanced swiftly at the jumble of startled faces looking up at her, leapt out again on to the street. She almost walked past the table and chairs parked outside the café. Then she stopped.

On one of the chairs, neatly folded, were a pale blue shirt, a cream jacket and a black pleated skirt.

Jenna picked them up.

Dad joined her from the shop next door. He stared transfixed at the bundle in her arms.

"Those look just like Mum."

"Yes, Dad." The familiar subtle perfume from Mum's clothes wafted through Jenna's head.

Dad pushed his glasses further up his nose. "That's what she was wearing this morning. I distinctly remember her ironing the shirt before she left."

"So do I."

"Where did you –"

"They were lying on this chair."

Dad grabbed Jenna's hand. "Good God! You don't think she's –" He couldn't bring himself to say the words.

Jenna made a huge effort to sound calm and collected. "Of course not." She stared at the drinking, chattering crowds in front of the Sloop Inn, envying their sanity. "She'd never do a thing like that."

"So where in God's name is she? Paddling naked in the sea?"

Jenna grasped his arm. "Don't panic, Dad. Let's think about this sensibly. Maybe she bought a new outfit, kept it on, had a cup of tea at this table and simply left the old clothes behind by mistake."

Dad shook his head. "I don't like any of this," he muttered. "It's not like my Lydia at all."

"Let's go down to that bit of the harbour." Jenna pointed towards Lifeboat House. "Maybe she went for a walk there after her tea."

They began to run again. Raindrops drifted into Jenna's face. The world looked blurred and watery. The harbour tide slapped and heaved against the sides of the wharf, snarling and energetic.

Mum sat on a bench, her back stiff and stern and upright, staring fixedly ahead, the rain glittering on her freshly permed and darkened hair. She wore new black patent-leather shoes with spitefully high heels, a tight orange skirt that barely covered her thighs, and a startling yellow suede cowboy jacket with droopy fringes. She looked bizarre and utterly unlike her normal self.

In her shopping bag lay two empty bottles of wine. She held a third, which she no longer had the strength to raise to her lips.

She looked up at them with bloodshot eyes as they stood, panting with relief, in front of her.

"And I don't want you *ever* to touch Benjie's room." She wagged a finger at Dad in admonition, as if she were half-way through a conversation with him. "*Ever.* I want it to stay just as it is. Just as he left it. Do you understand me, Elwyn? Am I making myself absolutely clear?"

"Yes, Lydia. Of course you are, dear. Now we're going to take you home for a lovely long rest." He gestured to Jenna. "Just stand up and lean on me. *There* you are. Slowly does it . . . We'll soon have you home."

Mum swayed on her new stiletto heels. "Don't wanna go home, Elwyn."

Jenna smelt wine on her breath, warm and sickly sweet. She turned her head away.

"I think you do, dear." Gently, Dad took her shopping bag. The bottles clinked. "Oh, yes. I think you do."

Jenna woke at dawn.

Somehow, somewhere, as she slept, the decision had been made.

She slid out of bed and sat at her desk.

She found a piece of paper.

Then she picked up her felt-tipped pen.

Her hand shook so much she had to hold it with the other one to keep it steady.

Dad said, "The doctor came this morning to look at Mum."

"What did he say?"

"He said it's depression. Understandable. She just needs to rest. It could last for a long time. We're not to expect instant results."

"But Dad, you've been up and down to her room today a hundred times. How can you possibly do that *and* everything else?"

"She'll get better. Strong as an ox, my Lydia."

That's right! Defend her, why don't you! In your eyes, she can never do anything wrong . . .

Dad locked the tea-room door, flicked the sign to CLOSED. "What she needs is a holiday away from here . . . Away from both of us."

Jenna kicked off her shoes. "You mean away from *me*."

A wave of sadness washed over Dad's face. "She'll come round."

"She might when I tell her what I've done."

Dad picked up a tray laden with dirty cups and plates. "And what's that?"

"I've written to the Head of Dance at the Academy." Jenna gave a bitter laugh. "Just what the doctor ordered."

Dad dropped the tray. Broken jigsaw-puzzle pieces of bone china leered up at them. Dregs of grey-brown liquid puddled across the floor.

77

"That's right, Dad. Smash! goes my whole career."

"You can't mean —"

Jenna's voice came toneless and flat, as if she were repeating a meaningless lump of useless information. "I've told the Head of Dance that unfortunately, because of a tragic accident in my family, for which I was entirely to blame, I shall be unable to take up my place in the autumn, and therefore she is free to offer it to someone else."

"You haven't posted the letter, have you?" Dad's face was ashen.

"I've done better than just *post* it, Dad. I sent it by Special Delivery. Dashed out to the post office for five minutes after the midday rush."

"So *that's* where you —"

"The Head of Dance will get it in the morning . . . By this time tomorrow, some other hopeful will be offered the chance of a lifetime." She bit her lip. "While all my silly little dreams and ambitions are lying in a heap, just like that awful mess on the floor."

In Benjie's Room

Jenna climbed on to the bus.

As it rumbled along the road out of St Ives she sat feeling as solid and heavy as a stone.

I'll never do this journey again.

When she reached Lelant she got off, stood for a moment outside the village hall.

Go on, girl, get on with it.

She pushed at the door.

As she'd hoped, she was early. Leah stood on her own in front of the platform, opening a parcel of ballet shoes and leotards, checking off the contents on a list.

"Hi," Jenna said.

Leah turned, her face lighting up. "Jenna! . . . Great to see you . . . Where's all your gear?"

"Before you say anything, you need to know . . . I haven't come to dance."

Leah's eyes darkened. "Sorry about that . . . Thought we could pick up where we —"

"No. We couldn't. I've given the whole thing up. There'll be no more classes, no ballet, no singing, nothing."

Leah's jaw dropped. "You can't be *serious?*"

"Perfectly serious. It's all over."

The door opened. A gaggle of four-year-olds burst into the hall, shouting, pushing and giggling, while their mothers hovered approvingly in the background.

"But why?"

Jenna raised her voice above the noise. "My mum's sick. Dad's not coping. There's too much to do." The words babbled out of her. "He's got to look after Mum and the tea room and everything. I must stay and help him. Full-time. There's no way I can leave him on his own and go to London. I'd never sleep for worrying."

"But can't he *hire* extra help? Someone else from St Ives? There must be —"

"No. He doesn't want to. He says there's not enough money. The Cockleshell has always been a family affair."

Leah grasped Jenna's arm. "I'm devastated. I don't know what to say."

"Nothing *to* say." Jenna stared at her extra hard, trying

to ignore the way her eyes stung. "It's not the end of the world, is it?"

"I can't believe you've said that, that you mean it."

"Oh, but I *do*." Jenna forced her mouth to curl up at the edges, when it wanted to crumple in a howl of pain. "I'm going to work with Dad until Mum's better. Then I'll find another job, in St Ives, or maybe somewhere else . . . What does it matter? Who the hell cares?"

Leah was being mobbed by little girls in pale blue leotards and frilly skirts, jumping excitedly around her, tugging at her hands.

She said, "*I* care . . . We need to talk this through. Can we meet tomorrow?"

Jenna shrugged. "Come to the Cockleshell if you like. I'll have my apron on and I'll be waiting on tables. Like hundreds of other people in Cornwall at the height of the season."

Leah said, "I'll be there at eleven . . . Please, Jenna . . . I beg you . . . Don't burn your boats."

"It's too late. I've written to the Academy. I've rung Aunt Tamsyn. I've told Helen. All my boats burnt in the harbour last night. Better than fireworks."

"I can't believe you're going to throw all your talent down the drain."

Jenna dipped her knees in a curtsy, like the one the girls always gave Leah at the end of a lesson. "Thank you, Miss Leah. I'll leave you to your class."

She pushed through the semicircle of four-year-olds. Once, she'd been exactly like them: hopping up and down, longing to dance, twirling and spinning, clutching Imogen's hand, hugging Morvah, frothing with excitement.

Not any more.

She wrenched open the door, let it fall shut behind her. She started to walk along the road, either side of her the summer fields of Lelant: on and on, the dying sun warm on her skin, the breeze in her hair, the dust of the road gathering on her shoes.

Nobody could see her tears and nobody heard her cry.

In Carbis Bay she stood wearily at a bus stop, wiped her face, waited until the bus arrived to take her back to St Ives.

Then she walked slowly down the hill, into the town.

I don't want to go home.

Dad will be clearing the tea room. He'll be hot and tired, too tired to talk. He'll need my help. Another pair of hands, that's all I am.

Mum will be shut in her room.

There'll be nothing for me but the same endless chores, day in, day out . . .

She glanced across to the harbour. The tide had been sucked out to its furthest point. The wet sand lay smooth and flat, glistening in grey-green swirls beneath the setting sun. Small battered fishing boats perched, surprised and waterless, like stranded fish.

She found herself moving into the harbour, across the sand, towards the soft, frilly edges of the sea.

I can't even bear to look at Porthmeor Beach . . . The pain of remembering what happened seems to get worse.

But in St Ives, there's no getting away from the sea . . . I'm surrounded by it . . . Porthminster Beach, this harbour, Porthgwidden Beach.

To get away from the waves that swallowed Benjie, I'd have to leave Cornwall . . . Maybe that's what I should do . . . Disappear out of everyone's life for good . . .

She turned to retrace her steps, her head down.

As she neared the shore, the scent of the town wafted towards her: the sharp, high stink of fish, the pungent oily smell of chips, meat pasties smouldering in their ovens, the seductive, sugary perfumes of Cornish ice cream and heavy slabs of fudge.

Suddenly, for the first time in weeks, hunger bit into her stomach, making her feel faint with longing. She could not remember the last time she and Dad had managed a square meal.

Promptly at eleven o'clock the next morning, Leah whooshed into the tea room, her cheeks flushed, her hair flying. She grabbed a corner table by a window.

She looked up at Jenna. "I can't let you do this, throw everything away, without putting up a fight. It's still not too late."

"It *is* too late. I told you yesterday —"

"Jenna, listen to me. You could ring the Academy. Tell them you've made a mistake. I'll ring them for you. I've spoken to the Head of Dance before. I'm sure she'd —"

"Tea or coffee?" Jenna asked doggedly. "And how about a fresh saffron bun?"

Leah flicked back her hair. "I don't want anything except five minutes of your time. Surely your dad will give me that."

Jenna's shoulders slumped.

"If you wanted to be a painter or a sculptor or a writer," Leah said quietly, so that the elderly couple at the next table, however much they tried, could not overhear, "I wouldn't be making such a fuss. You can paint or write at any stage of your life. But you want to dance —"

"*Did* want."

"This is me you're talking to, remember? You want to be a dancer and *you've only got one chance.* If you don't train now, if your body doesn't get used to the right exercises every single day of your life, *now,* while you're young, you won't be able to change your mind. Your body will have done it for you."

"*You* changed your mind."

"What do you mean?"

"You used to dance. For the last twelve years you've been a teacher. At some point in your career, you decided dancing wasn't for you."

Leah pulled Jenna into the chair beside her. "I didn't. The decision was made for me."

"How?"

Leah grimaced. "I was living in London, dancing the Sugar Plum Fairy in *The Nutcracker.* It was Christmas. I'd been shopping. I got delayed by the crowds. I was rushing like a maniac to get to the theatre. The lift in my block of flats was on the blink. I stabbed at the button but nothing happened. I was cross and late. I fell down the stairs."

"Were you badly —"

"It could have been worse. I damaged a tendon in my left knee. The pain was excruciating. I was told to 'rest' for three months, but even when I did, that knee never healed properly. I was thirty-two and I knew I'd given my last professional performance."

"I don't see —"

"The thing is, I'd given it my best shot. For fourteen years I had the career I loved and wanted. Every dancer dreads physical injury. When and if it happens, you move on to another career path: teaching or choreography or management."

"So?" Jenna knew she was being absurd, but something in her wanted to be so rude that it would make Leah leave her alone. "I'm moving on to waiting on tables."

Leah flushed. "*Really,* Jenna! If you can't take this seriously, I'm obviously wasting my time."

Jenna stood up. "Yes, you are," she hissed. "*Totally* wasting it. When you fell down the stairs, the only person you hurt was yourself. When I fell asleep, I killed my little brother."

Leah bent her head. "You didn't kill Benjie and you know it."

"Then *you* tell *me* what happened on the beach that afternoon."

Leah grabbed her bag. She stood up, looked Jenna in

the eyes. "I can't. Maybe nobody can. Maybe nobody will ever know. But I can tell you one thing."

"Which is?"

"That by ruining your own life, you're simply making everything a whole lot worse — for yourself and everyone around you."

She pushed her way to the door. Jenna followed.

In a way, I know Leah's right. But it's easier to keep her at arm's length than to let her know how I really feel.

They stood for a moment in the doorway.

"When was the last time you danced?"

"I can't remember," Jenna said. "I . . . I go into the studio and I can't move. I'm rooted to the spot, like a piece of furniture . . . Anyway, there's no point now, is there? I can stop torturing myself."

Leah reached up and kissed Jenna's cheek. "And I'll have to respect your decision. This has been very hard for me, Jenn. When you have a star pupil, you want to show the world . . ." She half turned away. "I'll let you know the results."

Jenna's mind felt cloudy and blank.

All she could remember was standing together with Benjie in this doorway. What was it he had said? That he was scared of something. Or somebody.

Of not being able to *see* properly.

Where were his glasses when he was found? Has anyone thought to ask? Were they washed into the sea before they winched his body into the sky?

She echoed Leah. "The results . . . Sorry, Leah. The results of what?"

"Your Advanced One exam." Leah turned back to her and frowned. "Don't tell me you'd forgotten!"

"No," Jenna said. "Course I hadn't."

"Are you all *right?*" Leah's worried eyes scanned her face.

"I'm fine . . . Really."

"You've lost a lot of weight. Are you eating properly?"

"Yeah, sure," Jenna lied. She gave Leah a brief hug. Through the tea-room window, Dad beckoned to her wildly. "Look, people are waiting to be served . . . I must go."

They were laying the tables for breakfast a week later.

Dad said, "Tamsyn's coming down to see us."

"Is she?" Jenna slammed a cup into its saucer.

"Thought you'd be delighted."

"Not if she's going to give me *another* hard time about turning down my place."

"I'm sure she won't." Dad fastened the strings of his

apron. "Anyway, I'm over the moon that we're working together." He hesitated. "Tamsyn says she wants to see whether Mum will go back with her, to London, for a little break."

Jenna bit her lip. "She'll have to prise her out of that room of hers first!"

"That's the whole point . . . I can't seem to get through to her . . . Like I told you, she's hardly eating, she's certainly not sleeping." He flicked aimlessly at a spotless table top. "I reckon if she goes on like this, she'll –"

"She'll *what,* Dad?"

"I dunno. Do something stupid."

Jenna said tonelessly, "Sorry, Dad . . . Mum's your problem, not mine."

Dad cleared his throat. "I understand."

But he went on flicking at the table, as if he wanted it to disappear.

Jenna sighed. "What is it, Dad? Spit it out."

"It's Sunday."

"Is that when Tamsyn's coming?"

Dad looked across at her. The nervous flicking stopped. "Yes." His face suddenly flushed, his eyes glittered with excitement. "I've planned the whole thing . . . Mum's birthday. The big five-o. I'm taking her for a special Sunday lunch at Porthminster Café . . . Booked a table and everything." He chewed at his lip. "Thing is . . . While we're out, I wondered whether you could clear Benjie's room. Not a lot, don't throw anything away, just tidy it so Tamsyn can sleep in the room comfortably without cutting her feet on toys all over the floor."

"But Mum said —"

"I *know* what she said. She'd drunk two bottles of wine, she was out of her mind. She hasn't been upstairs to Benjie's room since —" He whacked at a wasp which buzzed neatly away. "She'll never notice the difference, not if you're careful."

Jenna straightened her back. She stared out of the window at the faultlessly blue sky; at a boy on his skateboard, his face solemn and determined, rattling down towards the Digey; at a seagull standing on one leg, relentlessly pecking at a cobblestone before his throat heaved its unflagging, single-note call.

She said, "It's going to be another lovely day."

Not that I'll see any of it from in here.

The heatwave broke that Sunday morning.

Showers of rain lashed the beaches. Crowds of disappointed bodies scurried for cover. Gulls screamed into the sky. Cats crouched indoors on window ledges, staring out. Jenna bundled the washing off its narrow line in the courtyard.

Mum shuffled downstairs looking puffy and listless. She wore an emerald-green suit with a matching shirt which seemed to drain the colour from her face. A ladder in one of her stockings snaked its way relentlessly towards her knee.

"Do I look all right, Elwyn?" Pat, pat, went the hand to the hair. "I seem to have put on a bit of weight."

"Fine, dear, you look just fine . . . I love that colour on you." Dad beamed at her. "Doesn't she look wonderful, Jenn?"

Jenna slammed another ironed shirt on the pile.

"We won't be late." Dad said. "Pity about our open-air table. Looks like we'll have to eat under cover if this rain goes on . . . I've left you an avocado salad in the fridge, Jenn. One of my specials."

Yeah, sure, throw some food at me and hope it'll make everything OK.

The minute they'd left, Jenna switched off the iron, took a deep breath and walked determinedly up the stairs.

She pushed blindly into Benjie's room and shut the

door. The room was trapped in impossibly stuffy air, as if it hadn't been lived in for years. She threw open the window. Gulls circled the rooftops, eyeing her.

She turned and forced herself to look around the room. The space on the low table where the guinea pigs' cage had been loured at her emptily, covered in a film of white dust. Huddles of books, comics and toys littered every other surface. The insides of a radio spewed across Benjie's desk. On the floor, the train set stretched in elegant curves around bundles of crumpled clothes.

She bent to pick up a pair of Benjie's jeans, a favourite T-shirt; held them to her nose, pressed them against her face to push back the tears. She wanted to throw herself on Benjie's bed, call for him, magic him back from the dead so that she could turn to watch him: playing with the train, pushing parsley into Klunk's little face, tinkering with pieces of the radio.

It's no good. He's never coming back.

She stood up, her legs weak. Furious and miserable, she flung the jeans and T-shirt on to the floor by the door.

Just pretend this room doesn't belong to Benjie.

Pretend you're a cleaner in a hotel . . . You've got half an hour . . . Start by stripping the bed.

She pulled at the duvet cover, tore it off, hurled it

across the room. She lifted a pillow and stripped off its case. Then another pillow. She remembered the thousands of times on her way to bed when she'd pushed at Benjie's door to make sure he was sleeping peacefully, seen his fair hair and soft, round face, thoughtful with sleep.

She punched at the pillow and then began to hug it, murmuring Benjie's name, tears scorching her eyes . . .

Mechanically, she made up the bed with fresh linen, opened Benjie's cupboard and packed away the toys. On the floor of the cupboard sat the box for the train set. She unhitched the engine and the separate wagons, pulled apart each piece of track and stacked them in a pile.

She opened the box.

In it lay a small red notebook. She turned to the first page. Benjie had labelled it in his neat black handwriting.

This Diary Belongs to Benjamin Pascoe.
Top Secret!
Keep Out!

Jenna picked it up and sat back on her heels.

A vague memory niggled at the corners of her mind: of hearing a wild scrabbling, the closing of a cupboard, whenever she'd knocked on Benjie's door.

Was *this* what he'd been doing, hiding this away?

She wiped a grimy hand over her forehead.

A gull flapped on to the window ledge and began a long, excruciating wail.

The Diary

Jenna knelt on the floor for a long time.

Then, without reading a single word, she closed the diary, crammed it into her pocket, finished cleaning the room and hurtled downstairs, carrying a pile of Benjie's dirty clothes. She stuffed them into a black bin-liner and threw it away.

Rapidly, without tasting anything, she ate the avocado salad with a slice of Dad's crumbling wholemeal bread, clattered the dishes into the sink.

If I don't get out of this place for an hour, I'll go mad.

I'll take Benjie's diary to where he drowned and fling it in the sea.

If he had any secrets, I reckon they should be allowed to die with him.

She tugged on her trainers and threw a raincoat over her shoulders. Curled in his basket in the hall, Dusty watched her go with the merest flicker of curiosity.

*

The rain held itself softly in the air, like a filmy curtain.

Jenna began to jog: through the Digey into Rose Lane, down Bunker's Hill, along the Wharf to Quay Street, through Sea View Place and Wheal Dream to Porthgwidden Beach. She perched for a moment on a wooden picnic table, her heart thumping. Then she was on the move again, across the path above Porthgwidden, up the damp, grassy hill to the Island and St Nicholas Chapel.

From the top, she could see the whole of St Ives: its sprawling huddle of rooftops, the harbour and all three curves of beaches, the great wash of cloudy sky which the sun struggled to pierce. Miles of sea spread in front of her, blue-grey, full of secret life, its surface pockmarked by the mizzling rain.

She dug her hand into the pocket of her jeans.

She pulled out Benjie's diary and stood there, willing herself to fling it away, over the edge of the cliff, into the jaws of the sea.

She froze.

She remembered standing on the rocks, her shoulders burning, her heel bleeding, shrieking Benjie's name into the silent blue. How she'd have given anything to have heard him call, "Hi, sis! I'm over here!"

What if Benjie's accident and his diary are somehow connected . . .

Suppose the diary contains a clue to what happened to him that afternoon . . .

Don't I have a duty to read it?

She turned her back on the sea and took refuge from the rain against the low wall of the chapel.

Cradling her hand over the diary to protect its pages, she began to read:

<u>Monday</u>
We walked down the hill together after school, just G and me. I think she's very special. The others didn't notice. They went on ahead and left us alone. G always calls me Benjamin. I like that. I hate being called Benjie. It sounds so babyish. Mum calls me My own little Benjie. Yuck. Puke. Yuck.

<u>Thursday</u>
This afternoon we did work in pairs and I was a pair with G. The others started to giggle and point but I don't care. Now they giggle and jump out at us when we walk down the hill together. She says, Benjamin, take no notice. So I don't. As long as it's G and me together I don't care about them.

<u>Saturday</u>

We said goodbye on the corner of the street while Mum was in a shop. G is going away for Easter and I won't see her until next term. I'm very sad. I gave her a special present. She loved it. She put it on. She said, Goodbye, Benjamin. See you very soon. But soon feels like a long time away to me.

<u>Sunday</u>

I spent all day playing with Klunk and Splat, but all the time I thought about G. How she looked when she put my present on. How her eyes looked at me, all lovely and dark. I think she's beautiful.

<u>Tuesday</u>

First day back at school. I could hardly wait to see G again. But as soon as she came into the classroom I knew something was wrong. She wouldn't even look at me. She just pretended I wasn't there. I walked home on my own and I couldn't eat any tea or anything. Mum said, Oh, my little Benjie, whatever's wrong. I said, Go to hell, under my breath, but she didn't hear.

<u>Wednesday</u>

Everything is different. Something happened in the holidays. I don't know what. G won't be my pair any more.

98

She says she can't be my best friend. I said, Why not, why are you being like this? She wouldn't tell me. And she won't walk home down the hill with me. So I tried to pretend I didn't care. When I got home I came up here and broke all my new radio into pieces and trod on them one by one.

Friday

G has ganged up against me with the others. I can't believe it. After school I tried to tell Dad, but the tea room was full of silly people. I came up here and cried. I wanted to tell Jenn, but she was practising in her studio. She said, Go away, can't you see I'm busy, we can talk later. But when later came I was tired and angry. I didn't feel like talking any more.

Monday

They stopped me on the hill. All of them. I had to run to get away from them but then I fell over. My glasses came off and they laughed. I started to cry in front of everyone. I wish I didn't do that. It made them point and laugh even more.

Wednesday

They've got a new song. I hate it. When I hear it I feel scared. I don't know what they're going to make me do. They sing, Bye bye baby try, You must do it, Do or die.

Monday

P is the worst. Twins can be terrible because they are so close. They are the leaders now, the two of them. Teacher doesn't let them work in pairs in school but outside they are always together. It never used to be like that. I wish I had a twin. Together with my twin, we would fight back. Show all of them how mean we could be.

Friday

I wait for the others to go down the hill before I go home. Mum says, Where were you, why are you so late? But I don't tell her anything. Dad is always cooking and Jenn is always dancing. There's nobody I can tell.

Monday

They want me to do something really terrible. If I do they say they will leave me alone. I've said, no, I won't do it and I don't care about them. I don't care about anybody now.

Jenna closed the notebook. There was more, but she could not face it.

She looked across at the sea, suddenly hearing its roar, tasting its salty spray on her lips. A cold, solid anger gripped her heart, followed by remorse.

None of us were there for him.

Who are these twins who made his life such a misery?

Jenna suddenly realised with a shock that she'd known none of Benjie's friends. Mum hadn't exactly run an open-door household. When Benjie was home, he'd almost always been alone, in his room doing his homework or playing, or watching television in the living room. Occasionally, when Benjie had had someone round, Jenna's own punishing schedules had meant she was somewhere else at the time. Now, there was no one to whom Jenna could turn to ask.

Sunk in her thoughts, she hardly noticed the walk home.

In her room, she slid the diary into her desk, dreading the next instalment.

She climbed the stairs with Aunt Tamsyn and opened the door of Benjie's room.

"I hope you'll be comfortable."

Her aunt flung her small suitcase on the bed. "I'm sure I will . . . Everything looks extremely neat and tidy."

Jenna swallowed. "I cleaned the room this morning, packed Benjie's toys away. Dad asked me to. We hadn't touched it since —" She clutched at her aunt. "Will it get better, Tammy? I can't stand much more of this."

Her aunt stroked Jenna's hair. "I'll take your mother off your hands for a bit, give you and Elwyn a chance to get your bearings."

"You won't mind?"

Tamsyn gave a short laugh. "Look, I'll be working as usual. I'll give Lydia a key and she can come and go as she likes. In the evening we'll have a meal together and she can tell me how she's spent the day. I'll take her to a couple of shows in the West End."

Jenna said bitterly, "Lucky her!"

"Yes, well, it'll serve its purpose. She'll get over this black depression, I promise you. We'll have her back to work in no time."

Jenna moved to the window. Lights from the town had begun to pierce the rain in tiny showery sparks. "I'm not sure we will."

"What do you mean?"

Jenna shrugged. "Just a feeling . . . Benjie was the centre of her life. She's never liked me much. Dad's done his best to comfort her, but she uses him like a drudge. I saw them when they got back this afternoon. She looked bored out of her skull. He looked shattered. He made a real effort for her birthday: flowers, breakfast in bed, gave her a necklace he'd spotted in town, lunch at the Porthminster . . ."

Tamsyn said grimly, "She doesn't know how lucky she is."

Jenna looked across at her. "Too right. Mum despises Dad for loving her so much. Secretly she thinks he's a mug. She can twist him round her little finger."

Tamsyn flushed. "He deserves better than that. He's always been the most wonderful brother. He should have someone who loves him back."

"Yes." Jenna ran her tongue over her lips. "Do you know what I wish?"

"What?"

"That he'd find somebody else . . . Trouble is, my dad's not like that. He'd not even look at another woman, not in a hundred years."

That night Jenna took the diary from her desk and huddled into bed with it.

I've got to read the rest of this . . .

It's like it's burning into my brain.

<u>Wednesday</u>

The twins want me to steal from Dad's till in the café. They said it would be easy. Do it when he's not looking. I said, NO WAY. There's no way I'll let you turn me into a thief. They just laughed. They said if I didn't they would tell me to do something even worse. That I had one week to do it and then it would be something worse.

Friday

I don't want to go to school. I told Mum I felt sick. I stayed in bed. I didn't eat anything all day. I played with Klunk and Splat. I set up the train in a different way. I tried not to think of the song, but it goes round in my head. Bye bye baby try, You must do it, Do or die. Over and over in my head.

Monday

They wanted to know why I hadn't been to school for a week. They said they wanted to welcome me back. They said there was a note stuck on the door of my locker, but I wasn't to read it until I got home. After school I waited until they had left. Then I read it. It was gross. I tore it up and stuffed it down a drain in the road.

Wednesday

The twins caught me on the way home. They said I had one more day to get the money. I said, Go away or I'll tell Teacher. They just laughed. They said if I told him they would say I was making the whole thing up.

Thursday

After school they followed me again. They said they've got friends in their street who will come and beat me up. I was really scared. More than before. I went into the café. I hung around the till, but there were too many people. Mum said, Go and have some tea. I went into the hall and found her bag. Her purse had a lot of money in it. I took out one of the notes. I didn't look at it. I didn't know how much it was. I just shoved it into my pocket. Then I rushed upstairs to my room. I felt gross. Like dirty and mean. I'm sure Mum will notice. What will I say if she does?

Friday

On the way home, I gave the note to the twins. P sneered and said, Only £10! This isn't enough! This is peanuts and you are a monkey! I started to shout, It's more than enough. I don't know why I did it. There won't be any more. I won't do it again. No way.

Saturday

Only one more week of school and then it will be the end of term. I'll come home and it will be freedom! I can hardly wait. I hope I don't see the twins in the holidays, not even on the other side of the street. I never want to see them again.

Jenna closed the diary.

There were no further entries, there was nothing more to read.

Anyway, she had seen quite enough.

She switched off her bedside lamp and lay staring into the darkness.

Mum thought I'd taken that money . . . It never even occurred to her it might have been Benjie. I remember now . . . He disappeared from the table pretty fast . . .

I can't show anyone the diary. I've got to keep it private, for Benjie's sake.

But there's one person I could talk to. Eva Simons, the Head at Benjie's school. Bet she'd like to know what's been going on.

Those twins . . . Bastards . . . Pair of bullying thugs. Expect they were bigger and older than Benjie.

I'd bloody well like to know who the hell they are.

Tamsyn put down her cup.

"That was delicious, Elwyn. You still make the best breakfast in the world." She glanced across the table. "Doesn't he, Lydia? Have you ever tasted bacon fried to such perfection?"

Mum pushed her chair aside and stood up. "I'll just go and finish packing."

The room fell into thick silence as she left.

Dad started humming. Then he began to clear the plates.

"You're a diamond to do this for me, Tammy. Lydia seems really together this morning. Cheerful, spick and span. She hasn't been downstairs this early since —"

"I'll do my best with her, for your sake and for Jenna's." Tamsyn stared pointedly at her brother. "While Lydia's away, you will look after my one and only niece for me, won't you, Elwyn?"

Dad beamed at Jenna. "She's my one and only daughter, don't forget. The apple of my eye. And we make the most wonderful team now, don't we, Jenn?"

Jenna pushed her plate away.

"Oh, yes," she said. "We make a *wonderful* team."

After they'd closed the tea room and cleared up at the end of the day, Dad slumped at one of the tables.

"It feels really odd without Mum."

Jenna stood behind him, flung an arm across his shoulder.

"We've never been apart in all these years." He reached up and covered her hand with his. "You know we met here, don't you? She was on holiday —"

"Yes, Dad. You've told me the —"

"From London. Came in for a cream tea. We started chatting. Everyone else had gone. We sat over there in the corner, talking our heads off. Hester, old friend of mine — we were at school together — she was helping me, but she had to leave early. Lydia offered to clear the tables. I thought she was fantastic, so confident and polished and organised. We were a team from the start."

"Yes, Dad, I know."

He clutched her hand more tightly. "She will come back to me, won't she, Jenn? She won't suddenly decide she's had enough of all this . . . enough of me?"

Jenna slid her hand away. She sat opposite Dad and looked him in the eyes.

"I can't answer that."

"No, sorry, don't suppose you can." He made a brave effort at a smile. "But I'll always have my Jenn."

"Course you will." Jenna pulled off her apron and smoothed her hair. "Though not for the next hour . . . It's a bit urgent. There's someone I need to see."

"Oh? And who might that be?"

"Just a friend," Jenna said.

Dead End

Jenna hauled herself up the steep hill to Benjie's school.

I thought if I did this walk — as I used to do when I was younger, as Benjie did right up until his death — I'd feel closer to him somehow, be able to imagine more clearly what he had to go through.

In her head, the bullying twins were skulking heavyweight boys with short hair gelled into aggressive spikes and dark threatening eyes. They looked so alike that even their parents found it hard to tell them apart. At school they often used each other's names to make their classmates snigger behind the teacher's back. One of them carried a surfboard as if he intended to smash someone's head with it; the other held a £20 note which he stuffed guiltily into his pocket.

Jenna shivered.

It was late August and the school was still closed for the

last week of the summer holidays. No cars stood in the driveway. She remembered her own years there. Now there was nobody singing Cornish songs in the hall, fiddling with spreadsheets on their computers, drawing maps, flinging their bodies into indoor aerobics, learning about a balanced diet, whispering in the library, gossiping behind the bikesheds, jostling for lunch-time strawberry cheesecake, pushing out of the gates.

Or chanting songs in the playground:

"Bye, bye, baby, try,
You must do it,
Do or die."

She stood looking down over the cliffs towards the beach that had claimed her brother's life, trying to decide what to do. Bury her head in the same sand? Pretend she'd never found the diary?

I can't do that. I feel as if I was meant to find it, that I'm supposed to be doing something about it.

If I don't, who on earth will?

She held on to her bag more tightly. In it lay the diary, as if to give her strength.

I'm going to tackle the Head. She needs to know what's been going on.

*

The Head lived on Ocean View Terrace, in a large, double-fronted house perched high on the cliffs above Porthmeor Beach, five minutes from the school.

Jenna remembered walking there the day after Benjie's death, her feet dragging with dread; how the Head had already heard the news; how she had comforted Jenna and offered any help she could.

It felt strange to be standing on this doorstep again, as if her previous visit had happened years ago, in a different life. She forced herself to ring the bell. The door opened almost immediately: someone must have spotted her from a window.

"Jenna Pascoe? What a surprise . . ."

"Mrs Simons —"

The Head wore a simple long cotton shift. Her arms and face were deeply tanned, her eyes sparkled corn-flower blue. Jenna instantly felt dull and pasty, as if she'd spent the entire summer shut in a windowless room.

"Do call me Eva . . . Won't you come in? . . . Please . . . Take a seat."

In the large, airy front room, Jenna sank into a plump leather sofa.

I'd better soften all this with a bit of gratitude.

"You were so kind to me when Benjie died. I wanted to say thank you. I was in such a state at the time, I didn't manage to say it properly."

"I'm sure you did . . . You must miss him terribly."

"Yes."

Jenna's heart sank. She longed to tell Eva just how much she missed having Benjie around, how she'd give anything to be able to replay that fatal afternoon. They could have caught one of his beloved trains from St Ives to Penzance, or gone to the cinema to see the latest blockbuster – anywhere, anything but that beach.

She sat frozen, unable to find the words.

Eva filled the silence. "Everyone liked him, you know. I've only been Head at the school for a year – God, how it's flown – but I can tell pretty quickly how each class is panning out. There weren't many problems in Benjie's."

Jenna took a deep breath. She said carefully, "I think that's where you're wrong."

Eva gave a start, as if she'd pricked her finger on a rose's thorn. "Am I?"

"It's why I've come to see you." Jenna bit her lip. "You have twins at your school."

"Yes . . . Actually, we have *three* pairs of twins —"

"Well, one pair were gang leaders, intent on bullying Benjie. They made him steal money and give it to them."

"How do you —"

Rapidly, as if the words in her mouth were on fire, Jenna described how she'd found the diary. "Here, read it for yourself." She pushed it into Eva's hands.

Eva caught her breath. "Thanks, but I don't need to." She stared down at the forlorn red notebook on her lap. "Did Benjie *name* the twins?"

"No. One of them has a name beginning with P. That's all I know. If he *had* named them, I'd have gone to find them without involving you."

"Why? Are you out for revenge?"

"Yes." Jenna flushed. "No . . . I don't know, I haven't thought it out. I *don't* know who they are, so I'm asking if you do."

"I certainly do not. And even if I did, I couldn't possibly give you their names."

"I see. Then I'll have to find out who taught Benjie's class —"

Eva said quickly, "Mr Robinson. He's taken early retirement and moved away from Cornwall. A new teacher replaces him next week. Benjie's class have also left, Jenna. They've all moved on to different schools. Everything's changed."

"It *can't* have."

"Look, let's take a rain check. After the accident, on the Monday of the last week of term, I told the school in assembly what had happened. Some of the children had already heard. Everyone was devastated. Mr Robinson spoke to Benjie's class. The police also came to question them. Afterwards, I went to see your father at the Cockleshell –"

"I know you did."

"I told him. None of the children had been on Porthmeor Beach that afternoon."

"Some of them must have been lying. I want to talk to them."

Eva said quietly, "That's quite impossible."

Jenna leapt to her feet. "This is outrageous. There must be *someone* who knows what had been going on. Benjie said the gang made his life a misery. One week he even refused to go to school at all because he was too scared to face them."

"But –" Eva frowned, trying to remember – "we had a note from your mother saying that Benjie probably had a touch of flu."

"You mean you won't do anything?"

"Look, Jenna. We take bullying very seriously. I've seen how children can be wrecked by it. But I'm only responsible for them *while they're in my care*. I can't watch over them every minute of their lives, now can I?"

Reluctantly, Jenna said, "I suppose not."

Eva ran her fingers through her hair, the creases in her forehead deepening. "Benjie was one of the youngest in his class. Some of the children were eleven at the start of the school year, he was only eleven almost at the end of it. He was small for his age, and of course he wore glasses. But he shouldn't have been bully fodder. He was extremely bright, often top of the class." She hesitated.

"But what?"

"He was a secretive child. He never gave much away. If anything he seemed *super* confident, as if he were somehow cocooned in his own private world."

"So as far as you're concerned, the whole thing's over and done with?"

"I wouldn't put it as brutally as that." Eva's face had paled. "But yes, if you're pushing me, I must tell you my advice is to move on. Don't let his death ruin your life."

Jenna said bitterly, "It already has."

"What do you mean?"

"Nothing." She snatched at the diary, crammed it into her bag. "Thank you for talking to me, Mrs Simons. I must go."

Jenna flung herself down the hill and into town.

What a waste of time that was!

Stupid cow, with her big house, her rules and regulations, her successful career. God forbid anything should seriously disturb her life! I might have known telling her would get me nowhere fast . . .

I've done nothing but make a total prat of myself — and betray Benjie into the bargain.

Jenna stormed through the Digey and slammed up to her room.

She took the diary out of her bag, stared at its bright red cover, pressed it to her lips.

"I'm sorry, Benjie," she murmured. "That didn't get me anywhere. Mrs Simons refuses to cooperate. Mr Robinson has retired." Her back ached. "And I'm completely knackered."

She slid the notebook into her desk, propped it behind a history file she hadn't opened since cramming for her last exam.

"But I'm not giving up just yet. That friend of yours,

Hedley . . . The one who gave you Klunk and Splat . . . I wonder if —"

"Jenna?" Dad called up to her from the kitchen. "Mum rang from Tamsyn's . . . She sounded quite perky."

Jenna clenched her fists.

That's where I should be, settling in to Tammy's flat, getting all my gear together for the Academy and my new beginning. It's all so unfair . . .

Dad chuntered on. "I've made something special for our first evening alone together. Crab and coriander fish-cakes with asparagus, followed by sticky toffee pudding. Mum and I chose the same menu at the Porthminster."

Jenna muttered under her breath, "As if I care."

"By the way, just now, did you have a good time with your friend?"

Jenna grimaced at herself in the mirror: at her pale face, her tired eyes, her crumpled shirt with its slightly soiled collar, her wild straggly hair.

"Yes, Dad," she sang. "I had a wonderful time."

Jenna got half-way through the pudding and put down her spoon.

"Sorry, Dad. Can't eat any more."

"That's OK, Jenn. I did give you rather a lot."

"Dad . . . Klunk and Splat."

"How are they doing?"

"I caught Dusty sitting on their cage yesterday, trying to poke a paw between the bars. It's only a matter of time before he gets to them properly."

"They shouldn't be in the courtyard. I've been meaning to put them somewhere a bit safer for ages. You know how that cat prowls around."

"But it's cooler there, and I don't want to take their cage upstairs again. I feed them, but nobody plays with them any more." She swallowed a sticky crumb. "I think we should take them back to Hedley."

Dad mopped at his mouth with his serviette. "Benjie loved the silly little blighters."

"He played with them every day, took them out of their cage, let them scuttle around his room. I don't have the time. I'm sure there must be other kids who'd —"

"We can't get rid of them without asking Mum."

"For God's sake, Dad!" Jenna snapped. "Surely you can make a perfectly simple decision like that on your own!"

Dad's mouth twitched into an apologetic grimace. He pushed his plate aside and stood up. "You're right, course you are. Stupid of me to be so dithery and sentimental . . .

Call Hedley. Tell him we'll be round with them on Sunday afternoon."

Jenna lifted the guinea pigs' cage out of the back seat of Dad's car. She bent to talk to him through the window.

"You go, Dad. I'll leave them with Hedley. I'll walk home. I could do with the exercise."

Dad's eyes were bright with tears. "Bye, little fellas," he said.

Jenna watched as the car reversed and sped away. Then she turned, struggled up Hedley's garden path with the cage and rang the bell. There was no answer. She started to walk round to the side of the house. A tall, thin boy with wild ginger curls came running out to greet her.

"Hedley? Hi . . . I rang the bell but –"

"Sorry, everybody's out but me. I was in the garden." He took the cage from her and peered into it. "Wow! Haven't they grown!"

"Benjie loved them." Without the weight of the cage, Jenna suddenly felt almost light-headed, as if she'd been let off the hook. "He looked after them really well."

Hedley glanced at her. "Know he did. Klunk and Splat he called them. Used to talk to me about them all the time."

"Will you find a new home for them?"

"Sure. No worries." He hesitated. "I miss him." He bit his lip. "I'm really sorry about what —"

"I know." Jenna felt gangly and awkward, bereft of all the proper words. "Thanks." She grabbed at the opportunity Hedley had offered, took a deep breath. "Look, can I ask you something? It's about Benjie and school."

Hedley frowned. "What is it?"

"He was being bullied. Did you know about it?"

Hedley flushed. "There's always something crappy going on."

"So you *did* know."

"Sort of . . ." He refused to meet her eyes. "I kept well out of it."

"Who are they, the twins?"

Hedley gave a start of surprise. "Phil and . . ." He turned his head away. "You don't want to know."

Phil! He must be the P in Benjie's diary . . .

"But I *do*, Hedley. So one of them's called Phil. Who's the other one? Where do they live?"

Hedley shook his head. "I shouldn't have told you anything. Forget it."

"How *can* I? They might have had something to do with Benjie's death. I'm desperate to find them."

Hedley looked at her, alarm and fear flickering in his

brown eyes. "Please. Don't ask me anything else. It was nothing to do with me." He glanced at the cage. "I'd better go."

Jenna stepped back. Suddenly Hedley looked skinny and vulnerable. *Now it's me who's beginning to act like a bully!*

"OK . . . Thanks for taking them, Hedley. Thanks for –"

But Hedley had already turned away.

Slowly, Jenna walked from Carbis Bay into St Ives.

I'm back at square one. Maybe I should tell Dad . . . Maybe not . . . There must be someone I can talk to . . . Someone who could give me a clue . . .

When the GCSE results came out Dad gave her an hour off to go and collect them.

"Good luck, Jenn. Know you've done brilliantly."

She walked up the Belyars to her old school. The last time she'd done this had been for the history exam, her head throbbing with dates and facts and opinions. How simple and straightforward everything had been . . .

She'd done well: lots of As with a spattering of Bs. She crunched the piece of paper into her pocket.

The Head greeted her and shook her hand. "Congratulations, Jenna. How are you?"

She looked up at the kindly face with its bright, smiling eyes, felt the warmth of his large, firm handshake.

"Fine, thank you, sir."

"Good to see you again . . . I'm so sorry, more sorry than I can say, that we'll not be having Benjie here next month." He hurried on, "You must be so looking forward to London. New teachers, fresh start —"

"Oh, yes," Jenna said, too tired to explain. "I am." She glanced sideways along the corridor swarming with kids, suddenly filled with spur-of-the-moment courage. "Sir . . . do you have a minute? Is there somewhere we could talk?"

"Of course. My office." They pushed their way towards his room. The door clicked shut. "Take a seat . . . How can I help?"

"I've found out that Benjie was being bullied last term." Jenna's mouth was dry. *How many more times do I have to say that?* "I also know that a pair of twins were the gang leaders. They got him to steal money, made his life a misery. I wanted to know whether you had any twins who'd be coming to this school next term." Her throat felt sore, her heart heavy as lead. "One of them's a boy called Phil."

The Head stood by the window which overlooked green fields, his portly frame partly blocking the midmorning light. He looked down at her steadily.

"I'm almost sure I don't." He thrust his massive hands into his pockets. "But even if I did — I guess you know what's coming next."

"You wouldn't tell me."

"No. Don't go there, Jenna. Don't let the past burn you up into something bitter and twisted. You've your whole life ahead of you. Take the best of your memories of Benjie — and move on."

Jenna stood up, her eyes stinging with tears. "Easier said than done."

She left the office, shoved her way through the crowds of kids, walked out of the school for the last time, down the Belyars and into St Ives.

Right. That's it. I give up. That's the last time I talk about Benjie's bullies to anyone.

Leah rang her the following morning.

"They gave you Honours, Jenna." Her voice thrilled with excitement. "It's exceptional at such a high level. I hope you're as pleased as I am."

Jenna realised she didn't feel anything at all. Examinations, marks out of ten, bad, good, better, excellent. What on earth did they matter?

None of them brought back Benjie.

*

Imogen and Morvah came to the Cockleshell one after-noon, taking Jenna by surprise.

Embarrassed by her apron, flushed with the heat of the kitchen and the crowds, she found it hard to talk. She avoided their questions, took refuge in asking after them.

Imogen had been offered a job in a bank in St Ives. "Good promotion prospects – and I can actually earn some money at long last!"

Morvah was preparing to go to college in Truro. "A-levels first, then to university to study law."

When they left, Jenna felt crushed and mortified. She realised she had had enough: of the hungry customers, of the chores, of Dad's persistent, forced cheerfulness, his nightly singing of Mum's praises.

She remembered all the years of dancing for Leah, the joys of laughter and gossip with her two best friends. She knew those times had vanished. Everything had changed.

That night she climbed the stairs to her room.

There remained one final piece of the dead jigsaw she'd failed to snap into place. She pulled from the bottom of her wardrobe an empty case. Into it she crammed her ballet shoes, her tap shoes, her jazz boots, her tights and leotards, her headbands, two old chiffon ballet skirts, and a silver tutu left over from last year's charity show.

She carried the case down to her studio and kicked it into a dusty corner.

She shut the door behind her, locked it with an angry flick of her wrist.

And who the hell would bother if I threw away the key?

Towards the end of September, when the crush of summer tourists had subsided along with the heat, Jenna woke early one morning. In the cool light of dawn she decided.

It's useless, all this wallowing in self-pity. I must try to make the best of things.

Yesterday, she had had the beginnings of an idea. If she managed to pull it off, the results might just tempt Mum to come home and get back to work.

She took a quick shower and followed Dad down to the kitchen.

"Do you know what I heard a young couple say yesterday as they put their heads round the tea-room door?" Her wet hair dripped down her back.

"No, what? Chop some onions for me, there's a dear. They always make me cry."

"They said, 'This looks a bit shabby. Let's go somewhere else.'"

"Did they?" Dad reached for the sea salt. "Love this stuff. It's so much purer than the processed kind."

"Have you *looked* at the place recently? I don't mean dashed in and out of it like a headless chicken. I mean really looked."

"Can't say I have. Never got the time. As long as it's clean . . . Pass me the tomatoes, Jenn. And the parsley. Used to grow this in the garden when I was a lad."

Jenna persevered. "Clean isn't good enough, Dad. We've got competition. The walls aren't pink, they're dowdy. The paint on the window ledges has peeled in the heat. The front door's disgusting. The tables outside are thick with rust. We cover them with tablecloths when what we really need is new furniture. We should be tempting people to sit down, not putting them off."

Dad stopped stirring the soup. He stared at her, his wooden spoon dripping over the simmering liquid. "D'you know what? You sound just like my Lydia."

"What a thrill," said Jenna grimly. "How is she, by the way?"

Dad gave a watery smile. "Having a good time without me, by all accounts."

"Yes, well, *when* she decides to come home, we'll have a surprise for her, won't we? A Cockleshell she'll hardly recognise: white walls, a floor that's newly sanded and polished, blue woodwork, cream lamps and a couple of new paintings. Let's get rid of those horrible chintzy curtains and splash out on some modern white crockery."

"It'll cost a fortune!"

"Not if we shut the place and do the work ourselves. We could get the lot done in a week at the most. How about it, Dad? A whole new look for our Cockleshell."

Dad's eyes lit up. "We could tell Mum we did it to tempt her home."

"Exactly . . . She'll be so impressed with you. Come on, now. What do you say?"

Dad grinned. He turned to face her and saluted with the spoon.

"Aye, aye, Captain Jenn. When do we sail?"

She was up a ladder outside the Cockleshell in the warmth of the late-September sun, sanding down the top of a window frame, her mind, blissfully, a total blank.

Inside the tea room, Dad slapped white paint on a wall. He sang to himself, one of his off-key sea shanties that seemed to have no certain beginning and no particular end. Listening, Jenna realised it was not a sound she'd heard for many weeks.

Behind her she heard another voice, slow and husky.

It made her heart leap into her throat, though she did not know why.

The voice paused for a moment. Then it said, "Jenna?"

She turned to look.

Standing at the bottom of the ladder was someone she recognised, a face she'd seen before – yet she did not know his name.

"Jenna Pascoe? Great to see you again. We were just on our way to the shops." His face was tanned, his body tall and lean, his eyes dark. He wore an immaculate pale grey tracksuit with a white stripe framing the collar. By his side smiled a shorter woman with a face hauntingly like his own.

Jenna crawled clumsily down the ladder, aware that her jeans were covered in paint, her hair knotted into a grubby scarf, her hands grimy with dirt.

"I'm sorry, do we know each other?"

"Ah." He grimaced. "You don't remember me?"

Once again his voice seemed to tug at her heart. "I . . ."

The details of that panic-stricken afternoon washed across her mind more vividly than they ever had before.

Hesitantly, she said, "Are you . . . Did we meet when —"

"Yes. I'm Meryn Carlyon." He held out his hand. "I was one of the lifeguards on Porthmeor Beach . . . the day it all went wrong."

Meryn

"I'm so sorry." Jenna blushed. Meryn's hand felt cool and roughened by the wind and tide. "Of course I remember."

"It was a terrible afternoon. I wouldn't be at all surprised if you'd blotted the whole thing out of your mind."

"I only wish I could."

A frosty pause hung in the air like the first snowflake of a winter's day.

"This is my mum." Meryn slipped an arm round his companion. "I've been so busy on the beach I've hardly seen her all summer – and I've got a very guilty conscience."

"Pleased to meet you," Jenna said. "I'd have asked you both in for a drink, but as you can see we're –"

"Having an autumn spring-clean?" Mrs Carlyon said.

Jenna laughed. "That's right. We open again on Monday."

"Good." Meryn smiled back. Jenna saw relief wash over his face, knew he could see she was dealing with the pain. "Now the season's ended, my stint as a full-time lifeguard has finished for the year. Perhaps I could take you up on your offer next week?"

"I'd like that." Then she added, "Coffee's on the house."

"Oh, *well*." Meryn's dark eyes danced with laughter. "In that case, how could I possibly refuse?"

The Cockleshell rapidly began to show the results of their hard work.

"This," Dad said as they put the final touches to it on Sunday evening, "was one of the best ideas you've ever had. So glad you talked me into it."

Without their chintzy curtains, the windows stood clean and shining. The wooden tables gleamed beside the newly painted walls. The floor shone from its sanding and polishing. The room looked larger, brighter, infinitely more inviting.

Jenna gave a sigh of satisfaction. "Back-breaking but worth it . . . Nobody can call us shabby now." She glanced at Dad. "Have you told Mum what we've been up to?"

"Not yet." He straightened a new abstract painting on the wall. Rectangles of gold and orange nestled against a powerful sapphire blue. "This'll bring the sunshine in on a rainy winter's day. Bought it from Charlie's shop on the harbour. Cost me a small fortune but I thought, Hey, I'm going to look at it every day for the rest of my life, so I may as well like it!"

Jenna persevered. "So when are you going to tell Mum about all this?"

Dad clasped his hands together. "Why don't we keep it a secret from her? A kind of welcome home when she decides she's ready. I'd hate to hurry the healing process and Tamsyn tells me she's doing really well."

Jenna sighed. "If you like." She switched on the lamps at each table. The tea room glowed. "There! From grotty to glam in seven days. Reckon we can beat the other cafés in St Ives hands down."

Dad grinned across at her. "I thought of something else we could do."

"What's that?"

"Give the place a new name. We should call it Pascoe and Daughter. How does that grab you?"

Jenna's stomach heaved. *I suppose you'd planned to call it Pascoe and Son.* "Mum might not approve. I think we should leave it as the Cockleshell."

*

The refurbishments paid off immediately. The week that followed proved busier than ever, as all their regulars popped in to admire the new decor and stayed to gossip over endless toasted sandwiches and cups of tea.

Each day Jenna was aware of waiting for Meryn Carlyon to come through the door. Every time she disappeared into the kitchen with an order, she hoped to hear his voice on her return. Disappointed at the end of every day, she flicked the sign to CLOSED.

Expect he's forgotten all about me . . . Maybe he'll come tomorrow . . .

When she went to bed, thinking about him, she replayed the details of that fatal afternoon. She remembered the relentless sun; the exquisite turquoise of the sea and sky, mocking her darkening anguish; the sharp pain of her grazed heel; her burning shoulders; the terrible mounting grip of panic that seemed to freeze her tongue to the roof of her mouth; the blankness of people's faces, their shaking heads, as she'd asked the same question, each time more frantically, up and down the beach.

"My little brother's gone missing . . . Have you seen him by any chance? He's got fair hair and glasses and he's only eleven years old."

Alarmed by her terror, people swiftly checked that their own children were safe and sound, hugged them with relief. How jealous she'd felt of them.

She recalled the fear in the eyes of Imogen and Morvah as they slowly realised something had gone terribly wrong. How Imogen said, "I'm so sorry, Jenn. If I'd known you were worried about Benjie, I'd have stopped him wandering off."

And she remembered the moment she'd first seen Meryn.

He'd been the second lifeguard up at the hut. Quickly and calmly he'd taken down Benjie's details. He'd relayed them over the megaphone, his husky voice steady and precise; calmed her trembling body when she'd almost fainted; told her so gently not to panic . . . and then, all those dreadful minutes later, told her they'd done everything they could, that the incident was now out of their hands.

She remembered how Meryn had been stripped to the waist, wearing only the bright red shorts of the lifeguard. Fine dark hair rippled across his arms and over the lean firmness of his chest. His skin was burnished by the sun and wind to the colour of an autumn leaf.

Meryn Carlyon.

Had she sought him out on the beach, afterwards, the next day, the following week, to thank him and his fellow lifeguard? Had she bothered to think about him once during the nightmare weeks that followed?

She'd simply taken his help for granted, not given it a second thought. Yet that afternoon must have been almost as much of a nightmare for him as it had been for her.

At the end of the week, when Jenna had given up hope of seeing Meryn again, a battered postcard arrived for her: a photo of a fishing boat graced one side of it and a hastily scrawled message the other:

Hi, Jenna! Greetings from north Norfolk! A friend of mine works at a hotel called Captain's House in Cromer. I've come to stay with him in his fisherman's cottage for my last few days of freedom before I start a new job. But I haven't forgotten that coffee on the house.

Hope to see you soon.

Meryn

"Who's that from?" Dad asked, tying on his apron. "All I ever get is bills."

"Just someone I know." Jenna slipped the card into her

skirt pocket. "Would you mind if I left early this after-noon?"

"And where are you off to?"

"We've given the Cockleshell a face-lift." Jenna frowned at herself in the large new mirror they'd hung on one of the walls. "I reckon I could do with one too."

"You look beautiful as ever to me."

Jenna hugged him so abruptly his glasses went all skew-whiff.

"You would say that, wouldn't you? You're my dad."

She dashed to the bank and took out some of her savings. Then she walked resolutely into the hairdresser's.

"Don't cut it all off," she told them. "But I'd like a fringe for the first time ever, and take the rest to here . . . to shoulder length."

She shut her eyes. *Snip, snip* went the scissors as her hair dripped on to her forehead. With each *snip* she thought, *Out with the old and on with the new. New look, new me.* The results were startling. Jenna stared at herself in the mirror. Her face looked softer, her eyes darker, her mouth more clearly defined . . .

Delighted, she raced around St Ives. She bought three pairs of trousers and six bright, single-colour tops; new underwear; a wide leather belt; pink nail varnish, some new make-up, a bottle of perfume; leather ankle boots to match the belt; a bag to replace the one that, lying on Eva Simons's plush leather sofa, she'd suddenly noticed looked crumpled and worn; and a new loose cuddly red jacket, for when the nights grew cold.

When she got home, Dad said, "Wow! Is that my Jenna? I did quite a double-take."

"Well, I thought, What's the point in my having long, classic-looking dancer's hair if I'm never going to dance again?"

The glow of pride and admiration in Dad's eyes faded into pain. "Never say never," he said.

"Why not?" Her hair fell soft and thick on to her shoulders. "Because never is exactly what I mean."

As she flicked the CLOSED sign into place on Wednesday afternoon, Meryn Carlyon came running up the Digey.

He's here.

Jenna felt blood rising to her cheeks. Her end-of-the-day weariness fell away. She opened the door, feeling the damp October air brush against her face.

"Mr Carlyon! I'd given up on you!"

Meryn grinned. "I'm so sorry. I know I'm a bit late for

coffee." He stopped to catch his breath. "You've done something to your hair."

"Do you like it?"

"Very much. Makes you look older, more confident."

"Just as well. I can't grow it back as fast as I had it chopped off."

He laughed, peered over her shoulder. "And all this looks fantastic . . . You've transformed the place."

"Lots of hard work and a few good ideas."

"Look, I've just come to ask . . ." Meryn's eyes sparkled in the light of the tea-room lamps. "What are you doing tomorrow night?"

What do I ever do after work but collapse in a crumpled heap in front of the TV?

"Not a lot."

"Let's have supper together."

Jenna's heart seemed to skip several beats and then made up for lost time. "That would be great."

"I'll pick you up at seven."

"Where are we —" She could hear her heart thumping, prayed that he could not.

"I'll book a table at the Café Pasta, on the harbour." He glanced at his watch. "Sorry, must go. New job, fixing up new house share . . . Tell you about it tomorrow."

"Cool," Jenna said airily, trying to pretend she got asked out to supper all the time. "See you then."

And he was gone.

Can't wait . . . Twenty-six hours to go . . . Wish they would hurry by.

Jenna summoned up her courage.

"I'm going out tonight." She glanced shyly at Dad as they finished breakfast. "For supper."

"That sounds exciting . . . Anyone I know?"

"Don't think you've met him," Jenna said vaguely. Then, quickly, "Hope you don't mind."

"Mind? Why should I mind?"

"Because we usually . . . I mean, it's been months . . . I haven't been anywhere at night since . . ."

The unfinished sentence hung in the air like the smell of rotting eggs.

"Neither have I. What with Mum and this place and everything." Dad pushed his glasses further up his nose. "Matter of fact, thought I might spread my wings a bit myself. Hester . . ." He cleared his throat. "You remember I told you, she used to work with me here, before Mum arrived on the scene. Hester's been pestering me for ages to have a meal with her, catch up on old times."

"You never told me. Why haven't you been before?"

"Didn't like to leave you alone, Jenn. Not after everything that's happened."

"Well, call her, for God's sake." Jenna grimaced. "We've both been dancing round each other, haven't we?"

Dad grinned. "Just a bit."

"D'you know what?"

"What?"

"You're free to go out whenever you like!"

"Same goes for you, Jenn." He reached for her hand. "Same goes for you."

At six o'clock Jenna beat Dad to the bathroom by the skin of her teeth. She bathed, changed into her new trousers with a red V-necked top, brushed her hair until it shone.

She tried to remember the last time she'd had a date. She'd been to a party with Imogen and Morvah, when was it now? Easter! And then there'd been the party, Denzil's party, that none of them had gone to, the night that –

The day I met Meryn. Think of it like that, not in any other way.

I can't go through the rest of my life measuring what's happening against the day Benjie died.

For a brief moment she stood at her desk, pulled out Benjie's diary and stared down at it.

Benjamin Pascoe.

You'd have liked Meryn.

He'd have done anything to save your life, I know it.

I wish you could meet him now.

At the Café Pasta they sat opposite each other at a table by the window.

Jenna felt Meryn's eyes on her face.

Overwhelmed by sudden shyness, she looked away from him. "I want to say something I should have said a long time ago." She held up her hand as he began to interrupt. "No, hear me out. Afterwards, after Benjie . . . I should have come to thank you. You know, for your help."

"There was no need."

"There was *every* need. I can't think what came over me."

"It's called grief." Briefly, Meryn's fingers touched hers. "People cope with it as best they can."

"That's no excuse . . . It was a terrible afternoon for both of us, yet I never once thought what it must have been like for you."

"It was grim, of course it was. It always is, when something like that happens. I watched you dashing away with your parents, pushing through the crowds, and my heart went out to you. We still hoped that —"

"Don't remind me."

"Then me and the boys talked about the problems of those rock pools, how we can't see round the Island, whether we should have another lifeguard permanently out there."

"Could you?"

"We haven't the manpower. . . There are only five of us, and when Porthmeor Beach is as crowded as it was, we could double our number and that'd still not be enough." Meryn shrugged. "I sometimes wonder why accidents don't happen more often. Every day that passes safely in the summer is like a minor miracle."

"Just before you picked me up tonight, I made myself a promise." Jenna's eyes stung with tears. "That I'd never talk about the accident again, not to you, not to anyone."

"Why? Does talking about it make it any worse?"

"Yes . . . I can't stop blaming myself for what happened. But I guess . . . I *know* I must stop it, if I'm ever going to move on." Jenna turned her head to look out of the window at the harbour, twinkling with evening lights. "I've given up everything. My career, everything I really wanted to do. It's like I've shut myself into a box and now I can't get out."

Meryn sat back in his chair and looked at her.

He said, "We'll have to see about that."

They ate chicken risotto, leafy green salad, crème brûlée, talking all the while, as if that particular evening was going to be all they ever had. Yet Jenna knew there would be many more; that somehow Benjie's accident had linked them in ways that were very special, that would prove difficult to break. Talking about Benjie to Meryn had been easier than she'd thought it would be. She felt better, not more miserable, for having done so.

Meryn told her about his work. "For eight months of the year I'm a fitness instructor. I've just taken a job at Tregenna Castle, running their health club. For four months, in the summer, I work for Penwith Council as a lifeguard. Then it's back to normal life." He swirled the wine around his glass. "Well, kind of normal. I also work as a volunteer for the RNLI. It means —"

"You're a hero."

"Dunno about that."

"You're constantly on call, twenty-four hours a day."

"I feel it's the least I can do. My dad did the same. He gave his life to save somebody else."

Jenna gave a little gasp. "When?"

"Nine years ago. I was only twelve years old. Some fishermen came to St Ives, people nobody had seen before. I remember Dad saying they were using what he called 'a dog of a boat', he didn't like the look of it at all. While it was in the harbour he went to check on it. He warned them it needed a lot of repairs, but they didn't take any notice."

Meryn gave a bitter smile.

"This doesn't get any easier to talk about either . . . The fishermen were out in it one December afternoon. Glorious weather: clear skies, the sea flat as a sheet of glass. The fishermen had a huge catch. They pulled the nets on board and the whole boat went over. A ship spotted them and rang Lifeboat House. Dad was called out immediately. The fishermen were rescued – but Dad drowned."

"I'm so sorry –"

"Mum had three of us to look after: me and my two little sisters. They never found Dad's body, which made everything worse. Although we knew he'd never be coming back, we couldn't say goodbye to him properly. For months we went on hoping." Meryn's mouth puckered. "Every time I'm called out, I think of him."

"But you're putting your *own* life in danger. What if your mother loses *you* as well?"

"She won't."

Meryn gestured to the waitress for the bill.

"Enough of all this morbid talk. I want to hear about that career you say you've abandoned . . . And I've got something to show you."

"Oh?"

"I've just moved into an old cottage, right on the harbour, near Lifeboat House. Dewy, one of my best friends, he's getting married next month. His future father-in-law's buying him and Wenna a house in Carbis Bay, so he'll be moving out — and I'm taking over his cottage."

"Sounds wonderful."

"It does. It is." Meryn left money for their meal. Then he stood up and held out his hand for her. "Come and see it for yourself."

"I don't know about that," Jenna said shyly. "Maybe next time."

"Come on, Jenna Pascoe. Take one step outside that box you're in."

"OK." She smiled. "You've talked me out of it."

"Will You Dance For Me?"

They reached the bottom of St Andrews Street.

Meryn pushed at the front door.

"Come in. Dewy's off somewhere with Wenna, as usual, organising their wedding."

He took her jacket. A thrill of excitement, mingled with anticipation, surged through her at their first moment alone together.

"This place is old as the hills. Nobody's sure when it was built, it's just always been here. Our landlord made a fortune wheeling and dealing on the Internet. That's when he bought this, before all the dotcom companies went bust. Now he lives in California and leaves the running of the cottage to us – to people he can trust."

Jenna said teasingly, "I'm sure you make ideal tenants."

The cottage smelt strongly of mice, with the hint of sandalwood above it, maybe from scented candles.

"There's a bedroom and a bathroom on the first floor. The kitchen's down there, in the basement."

He led her through an untidy dining area and up a shallow flight of stairs. He turned on the lamps.

"There! Isn't it great?"

An enormous room spread before her, its ceiling arched with old oak beams. In one corner slouched a comfortable-looking bed, covered in a striped woollen throw; in another, armchairs slumped low and inviting. A huge fireplace held sweet-smelling logs. An old sofa sat facing a wide window which looked on to the harbour.

Jenna moved towards it and peered out. She could just make out the lights of a boat dipping far away at sea, a cloudless sky scattered with handfuls of stars; heard the soft grumbling waters of the ocean as they slapped against the wharf.

Meryn touched her shoulder. She wanted to lean back into him, feel his arms around her.

"It's too dark for you to see much now, but in the daytime you can sit here and see for miles. Sea, sky, sun, clouds, boats in the harbour, an ever-changing land-scape, sunsets to die for. Beats a boring TV programme any day."

Jenna murmured, "It's a fantastic room. It's almost like *being* on a boat."

"It is, exactly . . . Sit over there . . . I'll make us some coffee. And then I want to hear the story of your life."

Jenna drank the coffee. She told Meryn about her childhood in St Ives; how hard she had worked; how everything had gone according to plan until the day of Benjie's death; how, since then, her life seemed to have collapsed like a fragile house of cards.

I don't want him to think I'm a whinger. People who constantly complain are so boring. But the most exciting part of me has gone and I'm not sure I'm left with very much.

"You can't possibly give it all up." Meryn sat on the floor, leaning against one of the old armchairs. He drained his coffee cup. "All those years of gruelling work. They're irreplaceable."

"Could *you* leave your father if he was in the same position as mine?"

"I know exactly what you're saying, and the answer has to be yes." Meryn pursed his lips. "When my dad died, I thought I'd have to stay at home for ever to look after my little sisters and my mum. I'd have to become the only man of the house."

"And what happened?"

"For a time I suppose I was. Or tried to be. I was only twelve, for God's sake, but I did my best to be as manly and supportive as I could. Then one Sunday, Mum and I went for a walk together. She told me she didn't want Dad's death to make any difference to my ambitions."

Jenna shook her head. "You weren't responsible for your father's death. I fell asleep on the beach. I let Benjie wander off. It was all my fault. I've got to pay for it the only way I can."

Meryn said slowly, "Benjie wasn't a baby, Jenna. He was eleven years old. Nobody dragged him away from his crossword puzzles. He could easily have stayed where he was. He joined his friends because he wanted to — and then things went terribly wrong. Why do you have to pay for that with your entire career?"

"I just do." Jenna looked across at him, at his long legs stretched out along the floor, his bronzed face, his lean fingers as they held his cup. "I've made my decision and I've got to stick to it. There's nothing more to say."

"That's all very black and white, Jenna. The world is full of greys."

"What d'you mean?"

"There's never *one* answer to anything. Things change.

You can't set your future in stone because your brother is dead."

"You think that's what I'm doing?"

"Yes." Meryn put down his cup and scrambled to his feet. "Come on. It's getting late. I'll walk you home."

Jenna linked hands with him. "Thank you."

He drew her close, smoothed her fringe over her forehead. "On one condition."

Again, she wanted to dissolve into his arms, to be held and kissed and comforted.

"Which is?"

"That you come here to lunch on Sunday . . . You'll be able to see how wonderful this room looks in daylight."

"I'd love to."

"And you know what we'll do?"

"What?"

"We'll push back the furniture and you can dance for me. Anything, any of your routines — or maybe something new. That's it: I'll buy a new CD specially for you and you can improvise."

Jenna froze. "I can't!"

"I really want you to."

She shook her head. "Impossible. I haven't danced since Benjie . . . since July."

Meryn said firmly, "Exactly. So Sunday will change all that!"

"No," Jenna said. "*Nothing* will change all that." She pulled away from Meryn, putting a safe distance between them, forcing herself to stick to her guns. "My dancing days are over. If you don't understand that, you haven't understood anything I've said to you all evening."

"I see." Meryn looked crestfallen. "I'm sorry . . . I didn't mean to . . . you know, put my foot in it." He ran a hand through his hair. "Do you still want me to walk you home?"

"No, thanks," Jenna said. "I think I know the way." She turned to leave.

"What about Sunday?" Meryn called bleakly after her.

Jenna swallowed. "I'll be too busy," she said.

Jenna got home at midnight.

She tiptoed past Dad's room, then realised it was still empty. She hurtled her way upstairs.

In her bedroom she threw off her new jacket and gazed at her reflection in the mirror. Her face was flushed, her hair a thick tumble to her shoulders, her eyes wide and angry. Her head raced with the speed of her thoughts.

I said no and I meant no!

Who does Meryn think he is?

Comes breezing into my life, gives me supper, thinks he can wave a magic wand and make everything smell of roses.

Well, it doesn't. It stinks.

She sank on to her bed.

How can I possibly see him again?

I've blown everything before I've even given it a chance.

Dad and Jenna looked at each other across the kitchen table at breakfast.

Jenna said, "I didn't hear you come in last night. You *were* late."

Dad blushed. "Sorry. The time flew by."

"As long as you enjoyed yourself."

"Oh, I did." He stared at his plate. "I'll be out again on Sunday if that's OK."

"Sure," Jenna said, kicking herself for wanting to say the same.

Dad said, "So who's your secret admirer?"

Jenna blushed. "Is it that obvious?"

"Well, the new hairdo, the outfits, they weren't for me, now, were they? Not for your plumpish, frumpish old dad who never sings in tune!"

"Not exactly."

"Why are you being so mysterious? What have you got to hide?"

"Nothing. It's just that if I tell you, I don't want it to bring back all the memories."

"Memories?" Dad's face lost its happiness. "You mean of my Benjamin? How could it do that?"

Jenna took a deep breath. "I had supper with Meryn Carlyon . . . He was one of the lifeguards who helped us . . . who tried to find —" She looked into Dad's eyes.

He gave her the bravest smile. "I see . . . And I'm sure he did his best." He squeezed her hand. "Those lifeguards are the salt of the earth, Jenn."

"Meryn's dad drowned trying to rescue fishermen in distress. So he knows what it's like to lose someone you love." Jenna swallowed. "How's Hester?"

Dad stood up. "You know," he said to the teapot, as if it were an old friend, "after all these years, I reckon she's not changed one single jot."

The phone rang at midday.

Dad stopped singing. "Could you get that for me, Jenn? I'm making toasted ham and cheese for table four."

Jenna dashed to pick up the phone.

"Cockleshell Tea Room. May I help you?"

"Jenna? This is Mum."

Jenna's mouth seemed to be full of dust. "Hello, Mum. How are you?"

"Where were you last night? I rang several times to speak to Dad, but there was no reply."

"We were out."

"I see . . . There's a surprise . . . Where did he take you? Anywhere nice?"

Assume we were together, why don't you? That neither of us has friends who might just ask us out!

"Yes, thank you."

"Good. And how are you keeping?"

Well, I suppose it's nice of her to ask!

"Fine, thanks."

"Right . . . Good . . . So, is Dad there?"

No, he's sleeping on the moon and I'm running the Cockleshell single-handed!

"Of course he's here . . . Up to his eyes as usual. We both are."

"Could you put him on? I only want a quick —"

"No, I couldn't." Jenna's voice shook with anger. "He's busy keeping your one and only business afloat. He'll ring you back, *if* he can find the time."

She slammed down the phone.

I thought maybe she wanted to talk to me! Checking up on Dad! That's all she's doing . . . He's out for the first time in months and she's down on him like a ton of bricks.

"Who was it, Jenn?" Dad called.

Jenna said, "Only your precious Lydia."

"I'll ring her back."

"It's OK. I said you were busy." Jenna put her head round the kitchen door. "And by the way . . . Last night. Mum thinks we were out together. She kind of assumed . . . If she asks, you could tell her we had supper together at the Café Pasta."

Dad stopped buttering some toast. He blushed. "I could, couldn't I?" he said.

The week dragged by.

On Sunday Dad disappeared to Hester's, looking excited at the prospect. Jenna mooned fretfully around the house, unable to settle to anything, trying not to imagine herself back at Meryn's cottage, sunlight streaming in the harbour window, ballet music playing, Meryn watching her dance. As the afternoon wore on, she went for a walk along the cliff path towards Zennor, refusing to look down at Porthmeor Beach, refusing to remember . . .

I'm being stubborn as a mule . . . Well and truly back in that box of mine . . . Shut the lid and hope to suffocate.

But on Monday morning at eleven she walked like a robot into the tea room from the kitchen and was startled to find Meryn sitting at a table by the window. He grinned up at her.

"Hi . . . I've come for that coffee on the house you promised me."

Jenna blushed, overwhelmed with delight at seeing him again. "Of course."

"I missed you yesterday." Meryn gazed fixedly at the menu. "Half hoped you'd change your mind . . . Me and my stupid big mouth. Can't tell you how sorry —"

"It's not you," Jenna blurted out, surprising herself. "It's me. It's *my* fault. You were only trying to help."

Meryn grabbed at her hand. "Then come this Sunday. You don't have to dance . . . Forget I even suggested it . . . We can pretend I never —"

Jenna's eyes stung with tears. "But I *want* to . . . I'm *longing* to dance again." She clung to his hand. "It's just I'm terrified. I don't know if I can. I feel so stiff and heavy and scared . . . Terrified of dredging up all the memories, of pretending nothing happened to change my life."

Meryn stood up and took her in his arms. "I'll be there

for you," he said. "Nobody else will see. No one else need ever know."

At closing time, Jenna carried a long-handled broom, a pile of dusters and a can of lavender spray polish up to her studio.

She unlocked the door and switched on the light. The room looked dusty and pathetically neglected. Guilt clutched at her heart.

The last time I practised here was the morning of my Advanced One exam.

It was only July, but it feels like a lifetime ago.

I shut myself in here that night to wait for Dad.

I remember now . . . When he got back, we sat together on the floor for hours, not talking, just holding each other and thinking about Benjie.

Then he started to tell me what had happened at the hospital . . .

And then he burst into tears . . . He cried as if his heart was going to flood out of him . . .

I'd never seen him cry before, never felt the way the sobs racked his whole body.

All I could do was sit and hold him in my arms, tell him every-thing was going to be all right because he still had me and Mum.

Jenna wiped at her face with a duster.

Somehow or other I've got to summon the will, the determination to dance over that memory . . .

To heal its pain.

When the studio shone again, Jenna pulled her case out of the corner, opened it and chucked its entire contents on to the floor.

She threw off her working clothes, pulled on an old pair of tights and a black leotard. On went the ballet shoes. She checked her reflection in the wall of mirrors, feeling almost as if she were looking at a stranger. She raised her chin, corrected the line of her back and shoulders, tied her hair in a ponytail, leaving her new fringe in dark strands on her forehead.

She put on a CD and pattered towards the barre.

Gently now . . . very gently . . . half an hour only will be quite enough tonight . . .

I'll give myself a full hour's practice session tomorrow.

As she finished the last exercise, she realised that Dad was standing in the doorway.

"Jenna Pascoe! I turned off the TV and heard music coming from the studio . . . Then I thought it's been so long, I must be dreaming – maybe it's a ghost!"

Panting to regain her breath, Jenna gave Dad a deep curtsy. "Lots of very real flesh pounding around, struggling to get back into shape!"

Dad's face gleamed with surprise and delight. "My Jenna dancing again. There's a sight for sore eyes." He took off his glasses, polished them on his sleeve. "Why now?"

Jenna grinned at him across the room. "Because Meryn asked me to dance for him. I said I would. But it's going to take a week's practice before I'm anywhere near ready."

She skipped towards Dad and took his arm.

"Sit over there, in the corner, on that stool. I'll dance my exam routine for you — my ballet variations. Just to prove to both of us I can still get it right."

Dad's face lit up with his smile. "The perfect end to my day."

Sunday dawned grey and cloudy. Surfers raced down to Porthmeor Beach to tackle the heaving waves. Church bells clanged sporadically through the showers of rain. Jenna stood in the studio, practising at the barre, urging her stiff muscles to obey her meticulous instructions.

At midday, she ran through the Digey into Fore Street, down to the harbour and along to St Andrews Street. In one bag she carried her dance gear. In another — a carefully covered basket — she'd packed a selection of Dad's specialities: a freshly baked walnut loaf, six saffron buns, and a cinnamon and apple crumble.

She stood on the pavement outside Meryn's front door. The top half of the door had been flung open. Through it she could see down to the basement and Meryn muttering to himself, flinging a pan into the sink. The scent of roasting lamb filtered into the air.

She tiptoed through the door, left the basket of food on the table and sprinted up to the living room. It stood flooded with grey light from the harbour sea and sky. True to his word, Meryn had pushed the sofa against the wall and rolled up the scattered rugs. The wooden floor gleamed up at her invitingly.

She dashed upstairs to the bathroom.

Got to do this quickly, before I lose my nerve.

Five minutes later, she was down in the living room, standing in the middle of the floor, dressed in white tights and her special red leotard.

She heard Meryn climb the stairs from the basement, exclaim with delight at the basket of food.

"Jenna? Are these from you? Where are you? I didn't hear you come in!" He rushed up the shallow flight of steps. "Wow!"

Jenna blushed. "This is all your fault."

"You look great!"

"I've been very strict with myself all week . . . In my studio twice a day, morning and evening, warming up, exercising at the barre . . . Yesterday I could hardly move!"

"Will you dance for me?"

"Guess I'll have to if I want any lunch!"

Meryn grinned. "Amazing how the smell of roasting lamb can sway a girl's heart! I bought a new CD with you in mind . . . All the best bits from *Swan Lake*. Dance for me, Jenna. Let me see what you can do."

Jenna felt the rhythms of the dearly loved music flood through her body. They eased her nerves, softened her self-consciousness.

She kept her eyes on Meryn's face as she began to dance for him. Clumsily at first, gradually she gained in confidence. This coaxing of her body back to dancing life felt more important than any exam, any charity show – more important than anything she'd ever done before. She needed Meryn's approval. She knew from the look in his eyes that she had it. And as she danced, memories of the dreadful summer months wove through her mind: the cold pale dawns when she'd dreaded facing the day; her guilt and anguish as she relived special moments with Benjie; Dad's valiant attempts at cheerfulness; her mother's furious silence and contempt.

Life must go on, she made her body say. *Good or bad, it must go on. Every time I dance, I shall celebrate my little brother's life — and reinforce my own.*

"Thanks, Meryn." Jenna pushed her plate aside. "Not just for lunch. For making me dance again."

"If it hadn't been me, it would have been somebody else. I'm no expert, but you've got real talent, Jenna. I couldn't take my eyes off you."

Jenna blushed with happiness. "You should have seen Dad's face when he saw me practising in the studio."

"I can imagine."

"I felt as if — just a little — I was healing the hurt of . . ." She took a deep breath. "You know, of Benjie. Before, I reckoned the only way I could do that was by working beside Dad in the Cockleshell."

"So where do you go from here?"

Jenna shrugged. "I've no idea. I suppose —"

In the corner, the phone rang. Meryn darted over to answer it.

"Sorry, Jenna, emergency. Must go." He blew her a kiss. "Wait here for me. Back soonest."

He raced out of the door.

Jenna leapt to her feet, ran over to the window to look out across the harbour.

The dreadful warning thud of the maroons shook the Sunday air.

A Wedding

Jenna stood at the window, her heart thumping with fear. She watched as the offshore Mersey lifeboat trawled its way out to sea.

Meryn's on it, with his six other crew members.

Are they heroes or what?

Please, keep them safe among the waves.

She forced herself down to the kitchen to clear the plates from lunch, looking through the kitchen's porthole at every opportunity. She put the furniture and carpets back to rights in the living room. Then she paced up and down by the window, which was being lashed with rivers of rain, watching the heavy clouds scudding across the sky, the dark, ominous waters of the harbour at full tide.

I can't bear this a minute longer.

I'm going to Lifeboat House.

I'll wait for Meryn there.

She threw on her anorak, slid the hood over her head and grabbed her bag.

She hurried down to the harbour, the roast lamb and apple crumble lying heavy in her stomach.

The doors of Lifeboat House had been flung open to allow its massive boat to slide into the sea. The space behind it stood empty and bereft. Small groups of people huddled together against the rain, waiting for the return of their loved ones or simply hoping for good news.

Jenna felt suddenly very alone.

Dad was spending the day with Hester again, but she did not know where. Mum was in London, exactly where Jenna neither knew nor very much cared. She hadn't spoken to Aunt Tamsyn for a fortnight. She hadn't seen Leah or Helen for weeks. Neither Imogen nor Morvah had bothered to come to the Cockleshell again. Not surprising: she had hardly welcomed them with open arms. She'd merely asked them about *their* plans, deliberately deflecting attention away from herself, putting a new, icy distance between them. The rest of her schoolfriends had probably left St Ives for colleges and careers a long way off.

Don't let anything happen to Meryn.

He's made such a difference to my life.

Don't take him away from me . . .

An hour later, the Mersey lifeboat roared back on to the horizon.

Cheers went up from the bedraggled groups standing by the wharf.

Jenna blushed with relief and happiness, realising she was soaked to the skin but caring only that Meryn was safe and sound.

When the boat had docked, Meryn jumped off it. Jenna rushed straight into his arms.

"You're a nutter," Meryn said. "You're wetter than I am. How long have you been out here?"

Jenna's teeth chattered with relief and joy. "About an hour . . . I couldn't stay indoors a minute longer. I started imagining the most terrible things."

I want to kiss him, but not in front of all these people.

His eyes were misty as he looked at her. "You needn't have worried . . . It was what we call a FAGI."

"What the hell is that?"

"False Alarm with Good Intent." He pushed her wet fringe out of her eyes. "Go home and have a hot bath. I'll come to the Cockleshell tomorrow and tell you all about it. Go, quickly, before you catch your death."

She watched him flap into Lifeboat House in his huge oilskins to talk to the other crew members.

Then she turned and ran all the way home, wet as the sea itself, but as if she had joyful wings.

During the weeks that followed, Jenna felt that she was steadily climbing out of the pits of dead despair, and once more into life.

Every morning, before it grew light, she spent an hour in her studio at the barre. Two or three evenings a week, and every Sunday, she saw Meryn. Sometimes, if he was on late duty, she puffed up the hill to Tregenna Castle to swim in the health-club pool as his guest. Afterwards, they ate fish and chips on the harbour, washed down with steaming mugs of tea. They went to the cinema, raced home in the rain, sat warming their feet by the fire in Meryn's cottage. Often Dewy and Wenna were there, arguing about their marriage plans or the furnishings for their new house, discussing their wedding outfits or simply cuddling in a corner.

Jenna introduced Meryn to Dad, who was only too

delighted to make them soup and toasted sandwiches in his kitchen if he wasn't out with Hester.

Sometimes, when they were alone, Meryn would say, "Dance for me, Jenna" – and she did. Afterwards he would take her in his arms and thank her. "Couldn't take my eyes off you, not for a second."

One evening Jenna and Meryn walked hand in hand down the hill from the health club, slithering on the path's wet autumn leaves.

Jenna felt refreshed from her swim; her hair lay soft on her shoulders, her skin still smelt of chlorine from the waters of the pool. The fine November rain had stopped and the night sky glittered with stars.

Meryn said, "You know Dewy and Wenna are getting married here at Tregenna, don't you?" He tightened his grip on her hand. "Saturday week . . . I'm going to be Dewy's best man. My little sisters are so excited, they'll be two of six bridesmaids. My mother will be there – and I'd like you to come."

Lights along the path through the woods twinkled against the trees.

Jenna said slowly, "I'd love to. But I've got nothing half decent to wear."

"So buy something stunning."

"And what about the Cockleshell?"

"Surely your dad can give you the day off – or even just the afternoon. The ceremony doesn't start until three o'clock."

"I'll ask him tomorrow. He isn't going to like it."

"Use your best powers of persuasion."

"It's going to take more than that." Jenna paused before she said thoughtfully, "Though I might know someone who would fill in for me."

"There you are." He opened the iron gate for her at the bottom of the woods. They crossed the road and stood for a moment looking out on to the darkness of the sea and sky. "Problem solved."

"Don't know about that," Jenna said. "Problem aired might be a better way of putting it . . . Wish me luck."

Dad looked up from a pile of paperwork he was dealing with at the dining-room table.

"Our new decor is really pulling in the punters, Jenn. Usually there'd be a bit of a slump, mid-November, very few tourists, people saving up for Christmas. But this year for the first time we're busier than ever . . . Mum will be pleased as punch."

"I wanted to talk to you about all that." Jenna switched off the television. "Saturday week . . . I need the day off . . . and I'd like another one this Wednesday to go shopping in Penzance."

Dad frowned. "I can't possibly manage the Cockleshell without you."

Jenna flushed. "Then you'll have to get Mum back, won't you?"

"She'll come home in her own good time. I can't possibly —"

"What? You can't possibly do what? You always leap to her defence, every time!" Jenna shot up from the couch and darted across the room. She sat down opposite Dad. "When Mum left us in August it was supposed to be for a few weeks."

"I'm *aware* of that. She's been depressed. These things take time."

"Time for my patience to run out. Some friends of Meryn's are getting married at Tregenna. Meryn's going to be the best man. Yesterday he asked me to the wedding. I've accepted. I've got nothing to wear. I need to go to Penzance to buy a new outfit."

"Why do you need a whole day?"

"Because I do! I'm not flying back in time for the

lunch-hour rush. That's the deal, Dad. Like it or lump it."

Dad took off his glasses. He wiped his face with his sleeve. "There's no need to be so rude."

"Maybe there *is*. We've been treating each other like we're made of glass, like we'll crack up at the first angry word."

"I'm only trying to be –"

"I've done everything I could for you since Benjie died. All *you* can do is take me for granted."

"You know I don't."

"That's what it feels like, Dad. I work for you six days a week. I do all the chores, anything you –"

"I thought you *enjoyed* being a part of the business. We make such a good team."

"I *have* enjoyed it, in a way."

"Then stop sounding so resentful. Lots of kids would envy you, having parents who've built up a solid family business. One day, when I retire –" Dad slid his glasses back over his ears – "all this will be yours, Jenn. It's your inheritance."

"And what about your precious Lydia?"

Dad pushed back his chair. He ambled over to the window, twitched unneccessarily at the curtains. "Is this what all the fuss is about? You and Mum?"

"So what if it is? What are you *doing* to get her back? That's what I want to know."

"I can't do anything."

"Well, maybe I can." Jenna bent her head over her hands. "If Mum's not back here by Christmas, I'm going." She raised her head, looked at her father across the room. "Not just for a couple of days. I'll simply leave and get a job somewhere else."

"That's blackmail, Jenna." Dad's voice quivered with indignation.

"I don't care what it is." Jenna stood up. "Next Wednesday I'm going to Penzance. Saturday week I'm going to a wedding. You'll have to find someone else to do my job." She picked up the pile of invoices and waved them at her father. "This stuff has taken over every minute of my day. I want some of my life back, not for you, not for Mum, but for *me*. Do you understand?"

"Of course I do." Dad moved towards her. He threw out his arms in a pathetic gesture of apology and resignation. "I'm sorry. I didn't realise you felt so strongly. I'm a bit of a chump, aren't I? Can't seem to see what's under my very nose."

Something about the way her father stood there reminded Jenna of Benjie, of his vulnerable expression, the way his glasses reflected the light, the way his mouth used to turn down at the corners when nobody listened to what he was trying to say.

Her heart melted.

"Come on, now, you plumpish, frumpish old thing." She gave him a swift hug. "I've been thinking . . . Why don't you ask Hester to fill in for me?"

Dad gave a reluctant smile. "I suppose I could . . . It'd be quite like old times!"

"There you are, then." Jenna put down the invoices, straightened their clutter into a neat, organised pile. "And while you're talking to her, I've got another suggestion."

"What now, wonder woman?"

Jenna looked directly at him. "Why don't you ask her if she'd like a job three afternoons a week? To give me time to dance, do my own thing?"

Dad gasped. "What on earth would Mum say?"

"Does she need to know?"

"I couldn't possibly take Hester on behind Mum's back!"

"Couldn't you?" Jenna turned to go up to her room. "Think about it, Dad. In some ways, maybe you already have."

*

Jenna caught an early-morning train from St Ives to Penzance, staring at her fellow passengers and wondering how long it had been since she'd managed to escape.

Her February audition.

Too long ago . . . much too long . . . It felt like years, not merely months.

And just look at the struggle she'd had to get away from the Cockleshell for a few hours. Dad hadn't given up without a fight. Right up until yesterday evening, he'd put off talking to Hester, made every excuse not to ask her anything.

"Hester and I are such good friends," he kept saying. "What if she thinks that's all I want — for her to work for me again?"

"That's rubbish and you know it," Jenna said grimly. "Either you ask her or you will have to cope single-handed."

She'd almost laughed with relief when she heard him talking to Hester on the phone.

By the time Jenna got downstairs, Dad and Hester were already working in the kitchen. Jenna stood in the doorway to watch. Dad was talking to a small, slender woman with a mop of chestnut curls.

"The cups and saucers are still in that cupboard," he was saying. "Guess you already know your way around this kitchen blindfold."

Jenna said, "Morning. Pleased to see I'm no longer needed!"

Dad spun round. "Hester, this is my daughter, Jenna."

Hester gripped Jenna's hand. "At last! After all these years . . . I'm so delighted to meet you." A pair of bright green eyes met hers. "Elwyn tells me you've been an absolute godsend."

Jenna blushed. "I've done my best . . . I'll get some breakfast later . . . See you tonight."

Dad pressed an envelope into her hand. "Your wages, Jenn, plus a big bonus for being such a star."

In Penzance she bought a dark green velvet suit with long flared trousers and a short tight jacket, a white top with a sequinned edge, a pair of black shoes with a narrow heel and a small black leather bag.

She ate a salad sandwich for lunch with a latte and a slice of chocolate cake.

Not a patch on ours . . . But the best thing is not having to wash up . . .

She wandered through the shopping arcades, thought

about Christmas — about what she and Dad would do if Mum had still not returned.

On the spur of the moment, Jenna had threatened to leave Dad, get another job. Could she really go through with it?

I'll have to decide what to do if that so-called mother of mine stays in London, if Dad goes on letting her stay away.

The day of Dewy and Wenna's wedding dawned clear and mild.

Jenna could hear Dad and Hester clattering around in the kitchen. She flung back her duvet, realised she did not have to get up just yet, punched her pillow and went back to sleep.

At midday she had a bath, washed her hair, ate the lunch Dad had left for her on a tray. At half-past two, she came down to the kitchen.

"Wow!" Hester said. "Have you seen your daughter, Elwyn?"

"Give us a twirl." Dad's glasses were all steamed up. "You look a real treat."

Jenna climbed into a taxi and was whisked up the hill to Tregenna Castle.

"I'll meet you there," Meryn had said the night before

on the phone. "It'll be chaos. I'd better stick with Dewy to make sure he's got everything he needs."

Outside the hotel, in the courtyard, cars came and went in frantic succession. Crowds of people – couples, parents with gaggles of children, a few loners like her – stood in their Saturday best, many of them wearing flowers in their lapels.

Jenna walked shyly into the hotel. The wedding was taking place in a room on the right-hand side of the foyer, which looked out over the slope of Tregenna's gardens and then down to the sea. Hundreds of small chairs, covered in red damask, had been grouped in a wide semicircle around a table decorated with white lilies.

Jenna perched on a seat towards the front, directly on the aisle, on the right-hand side.

I expect Meryn's with Dewy in one of the wedding-suite rooms, making sure everyone's still sane! And I'm sure Wenna will be in a terrible state, with six bridesmaids to organise.

Within minutes the room had filled. Jenna spotted Meryn's mother sitting several rows ahead of her, remembered the moment they'd met when Meryn had first reappeared in her life. She checked her watch. Almost three o'clock. As she did so, Dewy and Meryn walked down the narrow aisle and took their places at the front.

Meryn looked round for Jenna. He gave her a broad smile of recognition and mouthed, "You look beautiful."

Jenna blushed.

As the music started, the guests got to their feet.

Jenna looked down the aisle for Wenna and her father, as they moved slowly up through the room. Wenna looked pale but happy in a ravishing long, lacy, cream dress.

Behind Wenna walked her bridesmaids.

All six of them.

Four toddlers, in pale pink satin, each clutching a single rose, trotted erratically behind the bride. They were followed by two taller girls, maybe twelve years old, dressed identically in the same pink, with the same flowers.

And almost identical faces.

Large, doe-like eyes, dark as Meryn's. Wide, smiling mouths. Small, flattened noses. Long, smooth foreheads reaching back to pale-gold hair, tied in thick plaits over their heads, and decorated with a single pink rose.

Meryn's little sisters.

They were twins.

Jenna gaped at them.

As she did so, one of the twins muttered under her breath, "Don't walk so fast, Phil . . . Slow down!"

*

The ceremony began.

Her legs trembling, her heart thudding, Jenna slumped on to her chair. Her hands felt numb with cold. She gripped them together and closed her eyes.

What if the twins who bullied Benjie were girls? Why has that never occurred to me before? How many twins called Phil can there be in St Ives?

She heard nothing of the words of the ceremony, sang none of the hymns, was deaf to the couple's vows. Her head bent, she stared blindly at the hideous patterned carpet, seeing little of Dewy and Wenna as they kissed each other's lips, hugged their parents, turned to embrace their friends.

She sat rigid as the guests burst into delighted applause.

Then she looked up.

She saw Meryn's radiant smile; watched him shake Dewy's hand, grasp his shoulder, touch Wenna's cheek and murmur, "Congratulations!" She saw him bend towards the toddlers to pat their heads; then hug each of his sisters in turn.

As he straightened his back, he looked directly at Jenna.

Unblinking, she stared across at him.

He beckoned to her.

She made no response.

The guests stood up, gossiping, chattering, laughing, smoothing their clothes, adjusting their hats, calling their children to order.

Stiff and silent, Jenna got to her feet.

She turned away from Meryn and walked to the bottom of the aisle.

She pushed her way through the crowd, across the foyer, through the open door of Tregenna.

Outside, beyond the courtyard, the gardens stretched languid and green. The clear sky blazed with stripes of icy turquoise and gentle pink at the start of sunset. On the horizon, the sea lay flat, smiling its strands of blue.

Jenna started to run.

Through Tregenna's woods, across Trelyon Avenue, down the narrow hill to Porthminster.

And on, down the firm wet sand of its beach, to the gently lapping edges of the sea.

The Photograph

Jenna took a deep breath, letting the scent of the sea fill her body.

She could feel the thud of her heart against her ribs. The waves curled around her shoes. Sea-water stroked the hem of her trousers. The wind lifted her hair on her shoulders, flapped her fringe away from her forehead. Her lips stung with salt.

Calm down, girl, calm down. Don't jump to any crazy conclusions.

Just because I've seen a pair of twins, and one of them's called Phil, it doesn't mean they knew Benjie or had anything to do with him.

Does it?

Why didn't I have the courage to go up to them, just now, and simply ask? Why have I taken the coward's way out and run away?

Jenna stared out to sea, to the calmness of the flat horizon, the beauty of the gradually darkening sky, whose pink had changed to deeper shades of flame.

Because they're Meryn's little sisters, that's why!

And if they were *Benjie's bullies, I don't* want *to know the truth . . .*

She began to walk again, up and down beside the edges of the sea. The tide sucked slowly out in lacy swirls. Like Wenna's wedding dress. She walked until her feet were soaked, her new shoes and velvet trousers ruined, her legs wet, her hands and face chilled by the salty wind, arguing under her breath.

Then she forced herself to turn away from the sea. She squelched as swiftly as she could back up the hills to Tregenna, summoned her courage and plunged inside.

The wedding room stood dark and empty.

On the opposite side of the foyer, the dining room was filled with lights, music, the clang of cutlery, the chink of glasses, the hum of voices and laughter.

She stood hesitantly in the doorway, looking at a pool of tables and waiters, plates, trolleys, faces eating, drinking, talking. Desperately, she tried to find Meryn among them. The bride's table seemed to be at the far side of the room. She slid quickly along its edge, her back against the wall, until she reached the top.

Meryn spotted her immediately. He leapt to his feet, pushed his way past the table towards her.

"Jenna! What happened? One minute you were there, the next —"

"I'm sorry. I must've seemed incredibly rude. But I had to get away. To think."

"Think about what? . . . Sorry, Jenna, this din . . . I can hardly hear you. And I've had two glasses of champagne." He grabbed her hand. "You're *freezing* —"

"I must talk to you."

"Come and sit down. I'll make a place for you beside me."

"I can't. I only came to say we need to talk." But she let him pull her towards a chair.

"There! Sit down and have a drink. Thaw out. I can't imagine what you've been up to for the last hour. You missed my speech. Think it went OK."

Jenna sank down, raised the glass to her lips, took a long gulp of champagne. The cool liquid set fire to her throat.

She said, as if it were a throwaway question, "Where are your little sisters?"

"Philippa and Gabriella? I so wanted you to meet them!"

Jenna's heart froze. *Phil for Philippa ... and now Gabriella ... Is she the G in Benjie's diary? Might I have found* both *of them at once?*

Meryn laughed. "They got a bit over-excited, poor little mites. They've been up since the crack of dawn. Mum's taken them home." He drained his glass. "But didn't they look gorgeous? And didn't they do well!"

Jenna's mouth seemed to have been stung by nettles. "Oh, they were brilliant."

"I'm so proud of them." He squeezed her hand. "Mum cried a bucket ... Do you know what I wish? The one thing in the world that would've made today perfect?"

"No, what?"

"That my dad could have seen them. They were only three when he died. How he loved them."

Jenna said mechanically, "I'm sure he must have done."

A waiter had brought a plate laden with smoked salmon and salad. Meryn slid it towards her. "Here, eat up."

"No, really, I couldn't –"

"Nonsense. It's delicious." He refilled her glass, then

his. The champagne fizzed and sighed. "There. Now, what did you want to say to me?"

"Oh, nothing, really," Jenna said. "It'll keep."

"Tell me tomorrow."

"Sure, tomorrow."

"Come round for tea . . . Give us both time to sleep in." Meryn waved his arm towards the sweaty band. They were sawing away at "Some Enchanted Evening" as a handful of couples bobbed and weaved on the tiny dance floor. "Aren't they wonderful?"

"Wonderful." Jenna pushed some cold, slimy fish into her mouth. It made her want to gag.

Some enchanted evening this *has turned out to be . . .*

Meryn gave a huge contented sigh. "Mission accomplished." He leant back in his chair. "The wedding went without a hitch. Dewy's a happily married man, they're off on honeymoon. We can have the cottage to ourselves." He touched Jenna's cheek. "Come and dance with me. Course, I'm a clodhopper compared with you!"

Jenna swallowed. "Could I have another glass of champagne?"

She sat on her bed, huddled into her bathrobe and woolly socks. In spite of whirling round the dance floor for what had seemed like a lifetime, she felt chilled to the bone.

Somewhere in St Ives a church clock struck two.

There must be some way of finding out whether Philippa and Gabriella are the twins in Benjie's diary.

The more I think about it, the crazier it seems.

Girls as beautiful and loved as they are don't become bullies. They don't threaten other kids for money. Huddle in groups and point and snigger and chant.

Not Philippa and Gabriella.

No way.

Yet she could not settle into sleep. She stood at her window, looked at the waning moon, counted the stars until her eyes ached and her neck grew stiff with watching.

Before she asked Meryn anything – and possibly made a complete prat of herself, said things he'd never forgive or forget – she needed some hard evidence that was nothing to do with Benjie's diary. A list of names, a document.

A photograph.

Jenna gasped. Why on earth hadn't she thought of it before?

At the end of the spring term, Benjie had come home

with a photo, a group shot of his entire school. Mum had said, "Benjie! You took your glasses off! My word! Don't you look handsome without them!"

If Philippa and Gabriella had been in Benjie's class, they'd be standing near him – or at least in the same row – in broad daylight. At least then she'd feel she had more of a cast-iron case.

That photograph. Where was it? Somewhere in Benjie's room? Would Mum have kept it safe, a treasured memento of her darling boy? If so, where would it be? Could she get into Dad's bedroom to search for it without him knowing?

She had until the morning to decide. No, she didn't. Her head buzzed with impatience. She must do it now. If she were quiet as a mouse, she could search Benjie's room without waking Dad.

She opened her door, tiptoed across the landing.

In Benjie's room, she flicked on the light.

Systematically she started to claw through his chest of drawers, his desk, his wardrobe, even underneath his bed . . .

Nothing. No photos of any kind.

Weary and heavy-hearted, she crept back to her room and drifted into a restless sleep.

*

"How was the wedding?"

"Oh, it was wonderful."

"Good." Dad slammed the oven door. Jenna flinched. "What's the matter? Have you got a headache?"

"No, honest, I'm fine. Drank rather a lot of champagne."

"Ah *ha*! Your first hangover! Well, I reckon that's what weddings are supposed to be about . . . I'm having lunch at Hester's. Hope you don't mind."

"That's fine by me . . . Have a great time."

The minute Dad had gone, Jenna raced upstairs to his bedroom.

If Mum had kept the photograph, where would it be? Under the bed in a suitcase? On the floor of her wardrobe? Hidden among her underwear in a chest of drawers? Jenna scrabbled everywhere. Once again she found nothing.

She crashed downstairs. There only remained the desk in the corner of the living room, where Mum had sat, week after week as a Sunday-night ritual, doing the books for the Cockleshell.

Jenna opened the flap. Nothing but invoices, cheque stubs, business records and two calculators.

She slid open the first of three drawers, then the

second. Nothing but paid bills, lists of their suppliers, VAT accounts.

But the last drawer Jenna could hardly open. It was crammed with photographs.

She pulled out the drawer, crouched with it in the middle of the room. Dusty yawned, stretched his long limbs and came padding over to take a better look.

The drawer was filled with Benjie. Hundreds of photos of him, as a baby, a toddler, a child – a ten-year-old. Mum must've kept every single shred of him that had ever existed. Sometimes he was with Dad and Jenna, sometimes with Mum. Mostly he was alone. There were none of him at school. None at all.

Jenna sat back on her heels.

Mum must have taken them with her to London, along with her other favourites!

Furious, her eyes stinging with tears of frustration, she shoved the drawer back into the desk. Recollections of childhood jealousy flooded back to her: Mum always seemed to be with Benjie, never with her. Mum's eyes lit up when she looked at her darling boy. However hard Jenna had tried, Mum never seemed to love her very much. Eventually, she'd stopped trying. She could always take refuge with Dad.

Coldly and deliberately, Jenna pushed the painful memories aside.

I've reached a dead end.

Or had she? Wait a minute. All those invoices, those business records. Somewhere in the piles must be the photographer's name and a record of payment. If she could find those, maybe she could track down the photograph at source . . .

The spring term had ended in early April. So Mum would have paid for the photograph in March.

Jenna opened the flap of the desk. Like a demented burglar, she began to rifle through its contents. Dusty curled contentedly around her legs.

Half an hour later she threw on her coat, stuffed the receipt she'd eventually found into her pocket and shut the front door.

She ran across the Digey into Rose Lane, past Church Place and Norway Square, down to the huddle of craft shops and galleries which lay beneath the terrace of the fashionable restaurant, Blue Fish. In the mild, end-of-November Sunday afternoon, people shopped for Christmas gifts; greeted their families; stood in friendly huddles on street corners. Someone was smoking a pipe: the refreshing scent of his tobacco floated into the air.

Jenna checked the heading on the invoice. Talisman Photography and Gallery. She walked around the shopping arcade until she found the gallery, tucked behind a graceful wooden archway. Its door stood open. Inside, a thousand photographs littered the walls, filled the display holders, lay on every shelf.

"Just browsing?" A voice came from a room behind the gallery. "Or can I help?"

"I'm looking for something very particular." Jenna stood at the entrance to the second door. "Are you the owner?"

A young man with a mop of untidy curls wearing a dirty overall stopped sawing at a wooden frame. He grinned. "I'm Alan Kernow, his son."

"Hi . . . Your dad . . . Would he have taken a photo of St Ives Junior School at the end of the spring term?"

"That's him. Does most of the local schools, given half a chance."

"Does he hold the negatives?"

"Nope. Gives them to the individual schools. Part of the package."

Jenna's heart sank. "So he wouldn't keep a copy?"

"He might do . . . There's another room full of his work through there. If he liked the photo, he might have framed it and hung it on a wall . . . It's worth a try."

Under her breath, Jenna said a quick but passionate prayer.

The room was cold, dark and slightly damp. It smelt of mildew and tar. Jenna shivered. She turned on the lights.

An Aladdin's cave greeted her. The grey stone walls dripped with photographs, each carefully labelled, although there did not seem to be any specific sequence or logic to their arrangement.

She began to search. Hundreds of pupils from many different schools danced before her eyes: small, large, enormous groups, some in uniforms, some in everyday clothes, some in colour, some black and white. All doing their best to stand tall, look smart — and smile for the camera.

On the third wall, her shoulders aching, her head throbbing with concentration, Jenna found her brother.

The staff and pupils of St Ives Junior School.

Jenna peered up at Benjie, her heart in her mouth, suddenly wanting to cry. There he stood, in the back row, almost at the centre, with his round face, grey eyes and sticking-out ears, his shy smile, the white shirt and dark green tie of his uniform.

Beside him stood one of the twins. Right beside him. Presumably this was Gabriella, her face calm and serious, her fair hair smoothed carefully into long neat plaits, her shoulder brushing Benjie's.

Jenna frowned. Where was Philippa?

She scanned the faces. There she stood, at the end of the row, her face in some subtle way more beautiful — but her eyes sparked with anger, her mouth turned down in a sulky pout.

As if she were furious that Benjie deliberately stood between her and her other half.

Jenna walked back into the gallery. Her lips tasted of mould.

Alan Kernow stretched up to hang another photo on the wall. He glanced over his shoulder. "Did you find what you wanted?"

"I suppose I did," Jenna said. "If you could call it that."

She tapped on Meryn's door. The top half of it had been flung open, as usual, as if to welcome her, but she could not find the courage to step inside.

Meryn called, "Jenna? Is that you?"

He pattered out of the living room, wearing the grey-and-white tracksuit she'd seen him in when she'd been up a ladder that morning outside the Cockleshell.

"Hi, Jenn! Don't stand on the pavement. I've just made us some tea. Come in."

"Thanks, but I won't."

Meryn stared in disbelief "But you must! We agreed we'd —"

"I want you to do something for me."

"What's wrong, Jenna? Something's happened. You're white as a sheet . . . Quick, come inside. Let me look after you."

Jenna almost sobbed. "There's nothing I'd like more."

"Then why —"

"Because I need you to find your sisters."

"Phil and Gaby?" Meryn blinked. "What on earth for?"

"I must talk to them."

"Why? What have they done?"

Jenna gripped the door. She found it almost impossible to say the words. "They were at school with Benjie. They knew him. There was bad stuff going on. Really bad." She looked Meryn in the eyes. "Phil and Gaby were leaders of a gang. They bullied Benjie. They forced him to steal money for them."

Her head seemed to fizz with dread.

"And I think they might know how he died."

Revelations

Meryn's eyes flashed with astonishment and anger. "What *are* you saying?"

"I have to talk to them. Alone."

"You can't do that."

"Why not?"

"Because . . ." Meryn was floundering. "I need to be there."

"*I knew* this would happen. You're on their side!"

"Of course I am." Meryn opened the bottom half of the door. "This is crazy. I've no idea what you're on about. You can't just stand there and accuse my sisters of all sorts." He stood aside for her. "Are you coming in or what?"

Jenna stepped across the threshold.

"Right." Meryn slammed both halves of the door and stalked up the stairs to the living room. "Take a seat."

Jenna crumpled on to a chair in the corner.

"Now." He stood looking down at her, his hands on his hips. "Are you going to tell me what this is all about?"

"No, I am not." Jenna dug her hand into her bag. "But Benjie is." She took out the small, red, battered notebook. "I promised myself I'd never show this to anyone again. But maybe you should sit down and read this."

Meryn closed the diary and gave it back to Jenna. He looked pale and shocked.

"I can't believe it."

"No. I didn't want to either. But it's there in black and white." Jenna stuffed the pathetic notebook into her bag, pulled the sleeves of her sweater over her trembling hands. "For weeks, I'd no idea who 'the twins' were. I went to see the Head at Benjie's school. She knew who I was talking about, but she refused to give me any names . . . Everyone's moved on to different schools since last term. Benjie's dead. I thought, This is crazy, I don't even know what I'm trying to prove. I'll just have to forget the whole thing." She clasped her hands over her knees. "Then, yesterday, out of the blue, I —"

"Saw my little sisters. Dressed as butter-wouldn't-melt-in-their-mouths bridesmaids!" Meryn's eyes burnt into hers. "So *that's* why you rushed off."

"Yes." A wave of nausea hit Jenna's stomach. *I can't go on with this. I'm going to be sick.* "I'm sorry. This is gross. I've put you in an impossible position. I'd better go."

"Don't be daft. We can't leave this hanging in the air."

"So what do we do?"

Meryn stood up. "Tomorrow I'll take the day off," he said decisively. "Ring my mum, tell her I want to spend some time with the twins. I'll collect them from school, bring them back here for tea."

"Will they tell you anything?"

"Give me an hour with them on my own. I'll sound them out."

"And then what?"

"Come round at five o'clock. We'll take it from there."

Jenna's eyes stung with tears. "I didn't want *any* of this —"

"Hey, course you didn't. We can sort this out." He held out his arms. "Come here."

She stood, comforted by the warmth of his body, muffled in his arms. "I'm sorry, Meryn. I wish it could all go away."

"You and me both, Jenna." He rocked her to and fro. "You and me both."

*

It's been the longest ever day at the Cockleshell.

Jenna struggled down the Digey under an umbrella. Rain snaked in gurgling rivers over the black cobblestones. She hadn't done any barre exercises since Friday and her body felt stiff and heavy. That afternoon, she'd kept getting people's orders muddled up and she'd dropped a tray of crockery. When Hester had come to fill in for her, she couldn't even find a smile.

Meryn took her coat and umbrella, led her down to the kitchen.

"I'd like you to meet my sisters." He threw an arm round her shoulder. "This is Philippa . . . and this is Gabriella."

The girls were clearing the table. Phil was slightly taller, her pale-gold hair drawn back in a ponytail, her eyes dark and resentful. Gaby's loose hair flowed untidily over her shoulders.

"And this is Jenna," Meryn went on, filling the uncomfortable silence.

With a terrific effort, she shook their hands.

I'm going to cut to the chase before I lose my nerve.

"Do you know why I'm here?" She looked up at Meryn. "Have you –"

"Yes. We had tea. We talked about Benjie." His grasp on her shoulder tightened. "Phil and Gaby say they know nothing about the bullying."

Jenna's heart froze. She looked directly at Phil. "Can you honestly tell me you never bullied my brother?"

Phil shrugged. "I've got better things to do with my time." Her voice was high and strident. "Boys are a waste of space."

Meryn said, "That's a daft thing to say. You'll think differently when –"

"When what?" His sister flushed. "I'm older and wiser?" She gave a bitter little laugh. "*No* chance. Dad left us. *You* left us . . . What's the point in loving people like you? You'll only get up and leave. You're all the same."

Meryn gave Jenna a worried smile. "I think we should go upstairs, sit down and have a proper talk."

"In your dreams!" Phil backed away from the table. "I've got homework to do. I'm off . . . Coming, Gaby?" She spat out the words. "Let's leave our so-called brother to Miss I'm So Perfect Pascoe."

"Now look here, Phil!" Meryn's voice shook with anger. "There's no need to be so rude."

But she had leapt up the stairs. The front door slammed.

Jenna looked at Meryn. Meryn looked at Gaby. Gaby bit her lip and stared fixedly at the floor.

Meryn said, "You don't really think I *deserted* you, do you, Gabs? I'm only round the corner. Any time you need me, I'd be with you in a flash. I'd never leave St Ives. Not in a million years."

Gaby looked up at him, her lips pale and quivering. "Don't take any notice of Phil." Her eyes filled with tears. "She's a liar."

"What?"

"She's winding you up."

"This isn't a joke. Why do you think Jenna's here? She's lost her brother. She —"

"I *know* she has." Gaby scrunched a fist at her wet cheeks. "Benjamin was my best friend . . . for a whole term . . . until —"

Jenna moved swiftly round the table. "Until what, Gaby? You have to tell us. This is so important."

"Philippa will kill me."

Meryn said firmly, "Oh, no, she won't."

Gaby pulled away from Jenna. "You don't know what she's *like,* Meryn. It's been three years since you left. You can't *imagine* how she's changed . . . How she can ruin everything." Her voice sank. "Especially for me." She sat abruptly at the table and looked up at Jenna. "I want him to go."

Jenna looked pleadingly at Meryn. "Do you mind? Give us half an hour together. This isn't about you. It's about Benjie and Gaby. Please?"

Meryn said, "OK. I'll make sure Phil gets home safely. Mum will be wondering where Gaby is." He darted up the stairs. "But I'll be back."

The front door slammed again.

"Here, wipe your eyes."

Gaby mopped her face.

"Let's sit upstairs. I want you to tell me what happened, from the beginning."

The living room felt chilly. Rain, driven by winds from the sea, hammered against the black sheet of harbour window.

Jenna drew the curtains. She put a match to logs in the grate, sat in a chair next to Gaby and held her hand.

"It all started," Gaby said slowly, "when Benjamin and I were asked to work as a pair in class. Mr Robinson thought Phil and I would do better with other kids . . . He was right.

"Phil's prettier than me — and she's always been the brainy one. She can read a book overnight that'll take me a fortnight. She's brilliant at maths. She helps me with homework. I used to depend on her. Then Benjamin started to help me too. Phil was jealous as hell.

"Just before the Easter holidays, Benjamin gave me a bracelet. It was only a cheap one, with lots of little charms on it. I thought it was wonderful, I wore it all the time." Gaby had started to cry again. "Mum took us to stay with Gran in Exeter . . . I went to have a shower one morning. When I got back to my room, I found the bracelet in pieces under my pillow. Philippa had smashed it up.

"I asked her why she'd done it. She said if I told Mum, if I ever had anything to do with Benjamin again, she'd stop helping me with my work, and she'd get all the other kids in the class to stop talking to me."

"Could she really *do* that?"

"Oh, yes. When Phil sets her mind to something . . . She had the whole class eating out of her hand. It's different now. We're at a school where some of the other kids are just as bright as she is. But at the Junior School, Phil and Benjamin were rivals at the top of the class." Gaby's voice darkened into bitterness. "But she was older than he was — and taller and stronger.

"The summer term was horrible. I had to pretend to

Benjamin that I didn't want to be his friend. I told Mr Robinson I didn't want to be a pair with him and he put me with someone else. Benjamin was shattered. He asked me where the bracelet was. Phil told him I'd thrown it away because it was cheap and nasty. He believed her. He just kind of seemed to give in — and give up. I wanted him to fight for me, to make a stand. To hit back at Phil when she cornered him. But he never did."

Jenna said softly, "Benjie didn't have a violent bone in his body."

Gaby gripped her hand. "I never wanted this. Last term was so awful I just wanted it to end, so Benjamin could get some peace. On the Friday, when he actually gave Phil that £20 note, I hated her for taking it, it was like the last straw. I nearly told Mum. I'd decided I was going to tell Mr Robinson, but by that time . . ." Gaby rolled Jenna's handkerchief into a soggy ball. "It was too late."

Jenna took a deep breath. In spite of the fire, the room felt very cold. "I have to ask you this. I know how hard it is, going over the past, but I have to know. Were you with Benjie on the beach the afternoon he drowned?"

The front door opened and closed.

Meryn ran into the room, bringing with him the chill

of the dark November night. His face and hair glistened with rain.

He looked at Jenna. "Well?"

Jenna released Gaby's hands, got shakily to her feet. "The story has been told. Thank you, Gaby. Thank you so much."

Gaby looked up at her. "What are you going to do?"

"Nothing. Hasn't it all been done? Benjie's dead. Nothing will bring him back."

Meryn put his arm round his sister. "I'll take you home . . . Will you stay, Jenna? I need to talk to you."

"Tomorrow." Jenna forced her lips to smile. "Tomorrow is another day. And maybe the sun will shine."

"Yes." Meryn frowned, his eyes anxious, his face pale. "Yes, maybe it will."

Jenna walked slowly into the rain.

She waved at Meryn and Gaby.

They waved back.

They went one way.

She another.

If Jenna had been awake on the beach that afternoon, this is what she might have seen.

Benjie all alone, sitting on the sand, poring over his crossword puzzles, sweating with concentration, his glasses slipping down his nose in the heat.

Gaby running up to him, calling him Benjamin. She'd spotted him in the crowd. She was supposed to be with a group of their neighbour's friends, celebrating a birthday. She'd given Phil the slip. Phil had a summer cold. Mum had kept her at home.

Benjie blushing with shyness and relief and happiness.

Gaby spilling out the words, fast as they'd come, faster than a torrent of rain, telling him everything. About the bracelet. How much she'd treasured it, worn it, even slept in it. Phil's jealousy, her foul-minded resentment. Plotting against Benjamin. Unforgivable. How sorry Gaby was and how ashamed. How she still wanted to be his friend – how she would *always* want to be his friend.

Benjie crouching in the sand, scarcely able to conceal his joy.

The group of other kids, Gaby's friends, none of whom Benjie knew, racing up to them, saying, "Let's all go to the rocks. Come on, we'll try to catch some crabs in the pools. Who can catch the most? We'll race you there."

And Benjie standing up, unsteady on his feet, what with

the sun and the crowds and his overwhelming joy, holding Gaby's hand.

For a moment in time, for the first and very last time, holding his beloved Gabriella's hand.

They'd been fishing, mucking about, among the rock pools.

Benjie caught a crab. Everyone cheered. He squealed as it nearly slipped from his fingers. Just in time, he managed to plop it into one of the other kids' jam jars.

"More!" everyone cried. "What did you say your name was? Benjamin Pascoe? Go catch us some more, Pascoe. Go catch some more."

Sun-struck, dumb-struck and love-struck, amazed at his new prowess, drenched in sea-water and joy, Benjie held his glasses to his nose and floundered on: over the rocks, round the vast craggy corner of the Island and then further still, into the deepest pools.

Trying to catch more crabs for Gabriella, trying to prove his worth.

"And then?" Jenna had asked, as the flames crackled and spat in the grate. "For God's sake, what happened then?"

"Someone pulled me away . . ." Gaby had choked. "One of the other kids said we'd gone too far into the sea, his dad was shouting for us, we had to go back to the beach immediately. Two of the boys picked me up and carried me to the shore, shoulder high, over the rocks, screaming with laughter. I kept trying to look round for Benjamin, but I couldn't see him. He'd disappeared behind the corner of the rocks . . . Five minutes later, we all went home. To light the candles on the birthday cake."

Jenna felt blood draining from her face. "But afterwards, the following week, at school. When Mr Robinson asked you, when the police asked you. You said that none of you were on the beach that afternoon."

"I lied. I had to. Phil knew I'd been to the party. But that's all she knew. She didn't know anything about us going to the beach. I was terrified of telling her I'd seen Benjamin, that I'd talked to him behind her back . . . She'd have been furious. I don't know what she'd have done to me . . . I know that sounds pathetic, cowardly. But I have to *live* with her . . . She's supposed to be my twin."

Jenna walked through the darkness of the wet streets, down to the harbour. Exhausted and starving, she bought fish and chips, huddled in a doorway to eat them.

Nothing's changed. Yet everything feels different.

I can see the last moments of Benjie's life.

A hungry seagull perched on a railing opposite her, eyeing her chips. She threw him some food. In a flurry of dark wings, a flock of birds arrived to demolish it. Jenna remembered the whirring blades of the helicopter hovering over the sea, their patient, insistent drone.

She flung the remainder of her meal into the air.

Slowly she stumbled back through the Digey, towards home.

Lights flickered in the living room.

I can't face Dad. I don't want to talk to anyone. I'll go in through the tea room.

She unlocked the door of the Cockleshell and locked it carefully behind her.

The tea room lay in darkness, the corners black, the tables bare, the floor swept, its windows waiting for the dawn.

From beyond the inner courtyard she could hear the television in the living room, Dad and Hester together, talking and laughing.

I can't bear to go up to my room.

I'm so wound up I feel I'll never sleep again.

No point in going to the studio either — I'm much too tired to dance!

She dropped her coat and umbrella by the till, kicked

off her boots, pattered into the kitchen to make a cup of tea, carried it through to one of the corner tables of the Cockleshell.

She pulled out a chair and sat down.

She switched on a lamp.

Its pool of creamy light glinted on the polished table top, filled the room with shadows.

And lit another shape.

Something in the corner opposite.

Someone in a hat, a heavy coat and leather gloves sat motionless as a watchful spider in a web.

"Hello, Jenna," said Mum.

On the Midnight Beach

"*Jesus Christ,* you gave me a fright!"

"I'm not surprised. You hardly expected me."

"You can say that again!"

Mum turned on the lamp at her table. "There! That's better. Now we can see each other properly . . . My, you've had your hair cut. *Very* grown up! Makeovers all round, I see. What about dear Elwyn? Does he look the same?"

Jenna ignored the question. "How long have you been here?"

Mum crossed her legs, pulled off her tight gloves, finger by finger. The scent of stale perfume wafted across the room. "Don't know exactly . . . About an hour?"

"And you've been sitting over there all that time?"

"Admiring the new decor."

"In the *dark?*"

"I rather like the dark these days . . . It's kinder on the eyes."

"Does Tammy know you're here?"

"Your aunt is in New York again, on one of her glamorous jaunts."

"Why haven't you told Dad you're —"

"From what I can hear, he's entertaining a lady friend. Thought I'd wait for her to leave before I announced myself. I wouldn't want to put him off his stride." Mum gave a sarcastic gasp, flattened her mouth with her hand. "I assume she is *going* to leave? That she hasn't taken my place in his bed?"

"That's a disgusting thing to say."

"I wouldn't *blame* him. I have been absent for rather a long time."

"You sure have."

"Who is she, by the way, the lady friend?"

Jenna said sulkily, "We're very short-staffed. She comes in from time to time, to help us out."

Mum's voice tightened. "*Really?* Not that girl who used to work here before I arrived on the scene? What's her name again? Esther? Nessa?"

"Hester."

"Right! Hester . . . I remember . . . Lovely chestnut

hair . . ." She lifted a bulging handbag on to her table, took out a packet of cigarettes.

"No smoking," Jenna said quickly. "The new sign's on the wall."

"I *see* . . ." Mum stuffed the cigarettes back into her bag. "You're not making me feel particularly *welcome*, Jenna. You haven't even offered me any tea."

"I wonder why!"

"You haven't touched yours either. Shall I make us both a fresh cup?" Mum heaved herself to her feet and strode into the kitchen.

Jenna screwed up her face.

Has she any idea how much Dad's missed her, how hard we've worked?

This being here unannounced, sitting in the dark, it's a deliberate game. She wants to catch Dad unawares, so she'll have something else to bully him about.

Maybe I should warn him that she's here.

"There you go." Her mother plonked two more cups of tea on Jenna's table. "New crockery, very trendy." She settled herself opposite Jenna. "Well, now, isn't this nice? Quite like old times!"

Jenna almost threw her cup of stone-cold tea into her mother's face. "Don't you even want to know how Dad and I have *been* since you left? It was August, remember? All these months, we've worked our fingers to the bone for you. Dad missed you so much . . ."

"Did he now? *Poor* Elwyn." She gave a meaningful look through to the living room. "Found it hard to manage on his own?"

Right! That's the final straw!

Jenna leant across the table. "You're nothing but a selfish, cold-hearted cow. Do you even *care?*"

Mum took off her hat, stroked the fake fur, patted her hair into place. She gave Jenna a look which froze her to the core.

"Not a lot," she said.

They drank their tea in silence.

China clinked against china. The new clock ticked relentlessly on the wall. Outside the Cockleshell, gulls shrieked in the rain.

In the living room, the television clicked off. Voices murmured faintly, then more clearly.

"Good night, Elwyn."

"Thanks for your help, Hester. Good night, dear. Mind how you go."

The front door opened and closed.

The silence thickened.

Dad started to sing John Masefield's "Sea-Fever", hopelessly out of tune.

"*I must go down to the seas again, to the lonely sea and the sky,*

And all I ask is a tall ship and a star to steer her by . . ."

He trotted across the courtyard and stopped. "Why are those lights still on?"

He came through to the door of the Cockleshell. "What the . . . *Lydia?* . . . Good God! My *darling* Lydia . . . I can hardly believe my eyes . . . When did you . . . How *wonderful* to see you . . . I'd no *idea* you were here."

"Hello, Elwyn. Could you take my suitcase upstairs?"

Jenna left them to it: her parents, sitting either side of the living room like strangers, Dad overwhelmed, wiping his spectacles on his sleeve, offering Mum some sherry. Mum sitting quiet, dour, holding the glass between finger and thumb, taking tiny sips with her heavily lipsticked mouth.

Jenna crashed up to her room, lay on her bed fully dressed, listening.

Voices droned on for an hour. A door opened. Mum's

footsteps climbed the stairs. Right up the stairs, to Benjie's bedroom. The door clicked shut.

Dad went to his room. There'd be no more singing tonight.

Jenna switched off her bedside lamp.

She lay staring into the dark.

Listening . . .

Something woke her: a tiny shuffling, like a hungry mouse in the wainscot, or a dove settling its feathers on the roof.

She looked at the luminous hands of the bedside clock. Midnight.

There it came again, the shuffling. A door clicked open. A floorboard creaked. Silence. It creaked again.

Jenna sat up.

What the hell is that?

She opened her door an inch, then further . . . then further still.

Benjie's door stood slightly open.

She tiptoed across the landing, pushed at the door with her toe.

It swung open.

Jenna whispered, "Mum?"

She dashed back to her room, wrenched at the curtains, flattened her nose against the pane.

Mum was walking briskly across the Digey as if she were on a shopping expedition to the supermarket. Across her shoulders flapped Dad's pale grey raincoat.

I must go after her . . . For Dad's sake, if not for mine.

Jenna hurled herself down the stairs.

Outside Dad's door she paused, heard his gently rumbling snore. She rushed down to the hall, pulled on her boots and coat. In minutes she had followed Mum: across the Digey, down to Porthmeor Beach and the roar of the pounding, tar-smelling sea.

The tide had sucked itself out. The sand stretched wet and flat, littered with clumps of weed. Mum was nowhere to be seen.

Where the hell has she gone?

She looked like a ghost, dressed in Dad's old clothes.

If she isn't on the beach, where else would she be at this time of night?

Jenna turned and retraced her steps, back to the Cockleshell. Mum had crossed the road, but instead of dipping down the Digey to the beach, she could have followed Back Road West along to Porthmeor Road. It led straight on to the Island.

Jenna caught her breath.

Was her mother trying to find the spot where Benjie had drowned? Instead of walking along the beach, was she simply heading up to the hill? To stand above those rock pools which had swallowed his life? In order to do what?

You stupid, selfish cow . . . In order to do what?

Her heart beating into her mouth, Jenna started to run.

Dim, sparsely placed streetlights hardly helped to clarify the swirls of Cornish stone, the darkness of lurking corners. Gates, paths, courtyards, walls, cottages – Crab Rock, the Bolt Hole, Neptune, Lower Deck, the Saltings – which in daytime she recognised like the back of her hand, loured at her, anonymous and forbidding, as if warning her off. The rain had stopped but the cobblestones felt slippery and treacherous. Moonless and starless, the sky hung low and threatening.

At the bottom of Porthmeor Road, she stopped to catch her breath. Tiny pinpricks of light shone from houses along the Man's Head ridge. Up on the Island, nothing beckoned but pitch dark.

Jenna began to climb, her feet skidding on wet grass, her breath frothing white-stranded into the dank night air. Gulls screeched around her, their privacy disturbed. She stared out to the sea, noticed how its darkness faded into grey at the horizon.

Cold with sweat and desperation, still further and upwards she climbed.

A pale raincoat flapped in the wind.

"*Mum!*"

Her mother stood at the top of the Island, her legs planted wide, like a scarecrow, looking straight ahead at the sea. She turned her face in Jenna's direction, stared as Jenna ran, panting, up to her.

"What are you *doing* here?" Jenna was so furious she could hardly speak.

"How did you find me?"

"Are you completely mad?"

Mum's eyes were blank. "Why have you followed me?"

Sweat poured down Jenna's back. "Why do you think, you stupid, selfish —"

"I can't talk to you, Jenna. Have the decency to leave me alone."

"Do you want me to ring the police?"

Mum laughed, a dour murmur of mirth that sent shivers of panic down Jenna's spine. "Where from? The Cockleshell? Go right ahead. By the time they get here, it'll be *much* too late!"

"For what? What on earth are you going to —"

"Join my own little Benjie, of course. Why else would I have come back? Didn't you guess?"

"No, of *course* I didn't! For God's sake, Mum! How can you even *think* of —"

Mum shrugged. "I can't face life without Benjie. Now get away from me and let me die."

She moved closer to the edges of the rocks.

Jenna grabbed at her sleeve. "I won't let you do it."

"Why not?" Mum had started to shake. "You go home and I'll jump. I can't even swim. You didn't know that, did you? The sea's so cold I'll be dead in minutes. What could be simpler than that?"

The wind ballooned into the raincoat. It seemed to rip at Mum's body. She escaped Jenna's grasp, leaving the coat behind. She toppled backwards, lay there for a fraction of a second, then slid clumsily over the edge.

Jenna darted forward. She screamed, "Don't do it, Mum . . . Don't fall any further." She knelt on the rocks. "Quick, hold on to my hand . . . There's something I must tell you . . . I know how Benjie died."

Mum clawed at the rocks, the tufts of grass. She raised her face. *"What?"*

"Please, Mum, hold on to me."

Mum flung an arm at Jenna's hand. Jenna grasped it with both of hers. "Find a foothold . . . Give me your other hand."

"I can't . . . It's wet . . . I'm slipping. . ."

"Give me your other hand . . . Right . . . Use your feet . . ."

"I haven't got the strength . . ."

"Push yourself up . . ."

"It's useless . . . I can't do it. . ."

"I won't let you go, Mum . . ."

"I can't manage it . . ."

"I refuse to let you go."

"I'm trying . . . Hold on to me, Jenna . . ."

"I've got you . . ."

"Please, hold on. . ."

Inch by painful inch, Jenna dragged Mum's heavy body back to the firm wet earth.

Mum lay there, racked with sobs.

She raised her face, her lips trembling and white. "This isn't just a trick to get me home?"

Jenna pulled her mother close, cradled her in her arms. "This isn't a trick."

"Why didn't you tell me before?"

"You weren't bloody well here to be told." Jenna pulled

Dad's raincoat across Mum's shoulders. "Here . . . Put this on properly before you *freeze* to death."

She pushed her mother's arms through the protective sleeves, wanting suddenly to hug the body that knelt beside her, to welcome her back to life.

"What happened to Benjie?" Lydia shook with cold. "How did —"

"Can we go home now? I'll tell you on the way."

They walked slowly back in the wind, down the wet, slippery hill, through the dark, deserted streets, Mum limping, Jenna supporting her, talking as they went, telling for the final time the story of Benjie's last few months on earth. And his last moments.

The words were easier to say in the dark.

Back in the kitchen they dried their hair and faces, climbed into pyjamas and bathrobes, sat at the table, their hands clutching mugs of hot soup. The colour returned to Mum's face, the trembling stopped, the look of death and desperation softened in her eyes, as if she were amazed and, after all, even relieved to be alive.

"Do you want to know the truth?" She looked across at Jenna, her eyes suddenly vulnerable. "Guess I owe you an explanation."

Jenna suddenly felt that she was seeing her mother for the first time, seeing behind the polished, organised shell to the woman beneath. "Only if —"

"What happened was very simple. You arrived too soon — and Benjie just in time."

"How d'you mean, too soon?" The soup burnt Jenna's mouth.

"Dad's told you how we met . . . But he doesn't know the whole story."

"You don't have to tell me."

"But I *want* to, Jenna. Just now, you . . . I nearly . . . Hear me out."

Jenna sat in silence, her eyes on Mum's face.

"I'd been dumped by a boyfriend in London. I was thirty-four and I felt utterly humiliated. I took the train to Cornwall, to recuperate, to try to forget about him. One afternoon I came to the Cockleshell, met Elwyn, helped him to clear up at closing time.

"Dear, reliable Elwyn: always so adoring." Mum looked away. "We had a summer fling, a holiday romance. But I knew he wanted more. When the time came to go home, and I realised I was pregnant with you, he couldn't wait to marry me."

Jenna burst out, "Did you *ever* love him?"

"Ah, Jenna, there are so many different kinds of love: companionship, security, affection. I'm *fond* of him. If Benjie had lived, I guess I'd have soldiered on."

"You said Benjie arrived just in time. What do you mean?"

"Elwyn and I had been going through a rocky patch. I was bored and restless. I'd seen a hotel for sale on Trelyon Avenue. I wanted us to buy it, make enough money during the season to take the winter off, travel, have some fun.

"Elwyn said he needed time to think. By the time he'd stopped dithering, someone else had bought the place. I was furious. I decided to go back to London, on my own. And then I realised I was pregnant again." Mum's voice dropped, her eyes misty with memories. "When Benjie arrived, he became my brave new world."

Abruptly, Jenna pushed back her chair and stood up. "There's something I think you ought to have. If it belongs to anyone, it belongs to you."

She climbed the stairs, opened her desk, walked slowly back to the kitchen.

She put the small, red, battered notebook into her mother's hands.

She watched as the tears fell.

Then she turned and crept up to bed.

Beyond the Waves

Mum did not come down to the Cockleshell until midday.

"She was exhausted last night." Dad tied on his apron. "We must let her sleep."

"Yes, Dad." Jenna piled crockery on to a tray.

Tell me the old, old story . . .

"She'll be recovering from the journey, getting her bearings, unpacking." He trotted into the kitchen. "It's so wonderful to have my Lydia home."

"I need to talk to Jenna." Mum hovered in the doorway to the kitchen as if she'd never set foot in it before. "On her own, Elwyn. Not for very long, but on her own."

"No problem." Dad closed the oven door, flushed and radiant. "When were you —"

"Could you spare her for an hour after the lunch-time rush?"

Startled, filled with foreboding, Jenna looked questioningly at her mother.

"Of *course*," Dad said happily. "Anything in the world for my two girls."

They shut the front door.

"Had to get out of there before I started to scream," Mum said. "Wouldn't want to scare off your devoted regulars!"

She took Jenna's arm. Jenna flinched. She could not remember her mother ever doing that before.

"The twins, the bullying, the diary, Benjie's death . . . Can't talk about any of it, Jenna. Never again. *We* know what happened. Let that be an end to it."

"Sure. I understand."

So what's this special expedition all about?

"God, I'd forgotten what the Cornish wind can be like!" Mum held on to her hat. "Shall we have a cup of coffee on the harbour? Get a bit of fresh air on the way?"

They sat opposite each other at the Café Pasta, at a corner table away from the window, safe from prying eyes.

They ordered coffee. Mum lit a cigarette.

"Thank you for last night, Jenna. And for not saying anything to Dad."

Jenna shrugged.

Mum flushed. "Wouldn't have blamed you if you'd been *glad* to see the back of me!"

Jenna said uncomfortably, "But not like that . . . never anything like that. Think what it would have done to Dad."

"Yes." Mum tore open a tube of sugar. It fell like brown rain on the froth of her cappuccino. "It wouldn't have been . . . appropriate. In the cruel light of day, I see that now . . . But –"

Oh, Jesus . . . I know what's coming.

"But what?"

"I am leaving. These last months, I've had lots of dark, lonely time to think, wandering the London streets, sitting in coffee shops, brooding in Tamsyn's flat. It's been a bit of a dress rehearsal, I suppose." She dragged on the cigarette. "I'm leaving Elwyn, you, St Ives . . . everything. But in a better way."

"I thought you might." The lump in Jenna's throat fell to her stomach. "You can't get over Benjie, can you? It's like –" She searched for the words – "you can't get beyond his death."

"No. You and Elwyn might be able to, but I can't. Everywhere I go in St Ives, people know me. I can hear them thinking, 'There goes poor Mrs Pascoe. She lost her little boy.' I can see the pity in their eyes. It burns me up. The house, Benjie's room, the Cockleshell. They're like a death trap. I must escape them to survive."

Jenna fought back tears. "If . . . when you leave, where will you —"

"Back to London." Lydia crushed out the cigarette. "I'll rent a flat in the suburbs, get a job in a West End store." Her eyes were sad. "Apart from Tamsyn, nobody knows me in the Big Smoke any more. No one at all."

"What about Dad?"

"He'll cope." Lydia leant forward to pat Jenna's hand. "I've given him the best years of my life. Make sure he won't expect *you* to do the same."

Jenna stared at her mother. "What do you mean?"

"Nothing and everything." Lydia drained her cup, buttoned her coat. "Shall we go back? I've got some music to face."

They stepped out of the Café Pasta on to the harbour. Bands of gold streaked the horizon, warming the cold grey-greens of the swirling sea.

Jenna remembered the day she'd told Leah she wouldn't be coming back. Sobbing her heart out on the road to Carbis Bay. Dragging herself over the harbour sands that now stretched ahead of her. How little she'd wanted to go home.

She longed for it to end: the grieving, the looking back, prodding at the past. She felt a desperate longing to move on; knew suddenly she had come to the end of the line.

Lydia took her arm again, but this time Jenna pulled away.

"I'm taking the rest of the day off. You can help Dad in the Cockleshell. It'll give you time to talk." She swallowed. "I'd rather *not* be around."

Lydia gave a start of surprise. "Where are you —"

"To see a friend." Jenna wound her scarf more tightly. "We might have supper together." She looked her mother in the eyes. "Don't wait up for me."

Lydia held out her hand. "I'll be leaving soon, Jenna. No point prolonging the agony. Tomorrow, I may not get a proper chance to say goodbye." She moistened her lips. "I want to wish you luck. When I'm settled in London, perhaps we could meet?"

Jenna took her mother's hand, as if she were accepting a peace offering.

After all these years, she's calling a truce.

She summoned every ounce of her composure. "Perhaps."

And then she turned away.

*

She started to walk: fast, determined, purposeful. Along the harbour towards Lifeboat House, up St Andrews Street, past the huddles of cottages — Beachside, Driftwood, Chimneys, Blue Mist — up to the brow of the hill.

She began to run. Towards Tregenna's woods, through the gate, past the splashing fountain, on through the trees to the Castle. She crashed into the foyer, raced past a startled receptionist, along the corridor and down the flight of stairs.

One of the staff sat at the health-club desk.

"Just come to see Meryn," Jenna gasped.

She pushed through the doors into the stuffy heat of the gym, up the wet, heavy-slabbed steps, into the cool glass dome of the swimming pool.

Meryn crouched at the edge of the pool, watching a young woman swim towards him. "That's it, Lois! Good girl! You've done it . . . It's all about confidence, isn't it?"

He looked up, startled, as Jenna raced into his arms.

"Hi! What a wonderful surprise . . . Gaby told me everything as we walked home. I had a spectacular row with Phil —"

But it's all too late . . .

"Really hauled her over the coals. She's sorry, Jenna."

Everything's breaking up . . .

"Really sorry . . . and so am I." He hugged her closer, felt her body shaking with sobs. "Jenna? My darling girl . . . Here, come and sit down."

Back in Meryn's cottage, they lay quietly in each other's arms.

The fire flickered the other side of the room.

"I'm glad you came to find me," Meryn said. "All those tears . . . Thought they would never stop."

Jenna raised her face to look at him. "I've had to be so strong . . . to face the twins, talk to Gaby, cope with Mum, make her see sense, tell her about Benjie, give her the diary. And then listen to her tell me she's leaving us for good."

She ran her fingers over Meryn's cheekbone, down his chin to the hollow of his neck.

"I thought, I can't take any more: other people's cruelty, other people's problems."

Meryn drew her closer.

"No more tears, I promise . . ." Her voice choked over the words. "Kiss me again."

But as he did so, Jenna knew that a chapter in her life had closed.

*

Early next morning, a taxi arrived for Lydia and drove her away.

Dad stared at the empty road. "It's only a matter of time," he said. "She'll be back."

But his face was pale, his voice lacked conviction, and he couldn't meet Jenna's eyes.

"Of course, Dad. She'll be back."

And pigs might fly.

But her heart went out to him.

All day they worked on automatic pilot, piling dirty dishes in the sink, heating soup, cutting bread for toast, making endless pots of tea. Jenna longed for Dad's tuneless singing, but the pots and pans rang coldly to the sound of silence.

Over supper, Jenna said, "Next week, do you think Hester could cover for me?"

"How long for?" Behind his glasses, Dad's eyes flashed with fear. "You're not leaving me too?"

Jenna leant forward to grip his hand, shocked by how cold he felt.

"I want to stay with Tammy. I rang her this morning. She got back from New York last night. Please, Dad, may I? Just for a couple of days."

*

At Paddington she caught a taxi.

It's half-past two . . . I'd better go straight there before I lose my nerve . . .

"Could you take me to the Urdang at Finsbury Town Hall, please?"

The cab wove bumpily through the crowded London streets.

Stick to your guns, girl . . . Tell it like it is.

Jenna stood rooted to the pavement as the taxi lurched away.

In front of her stretched a long, red-brick Victorian building, utterly unlike anything she had ever seen before. Two storeys high, its walls were set with tall, graceful stained-glass windows that seemed to peer down at her expectantly.

Her heart missed a beat.

Then she took a deep breath and crossed the road.

Inside, she said to the receptionist, "I'm so sorry, but I haven't got an appointment. I've come all the way from Cornwall. Could the Head of Dance see me? Just for ten minutes? There's something terribly important I need to tell her. Please?"

Phone calls were made. Jenna hopped up and down, trying to take in the size and spaciousness of the building.

The receptionist smiled. "The Head of Dance will see you. Go up the first flight of stairs and turn left. Her office is at the end of the corridor. Wait outside until she calls you in."

"*Thank* you." Jenna squeaked. She turned to face the stairs, willing her trembling knees to climb the cold marble steps.

She reached the first floor — and stood transfixed.

Through the corridor windows on her right she saw a vast hall, filled with lights. Mirrors with glittering frames hung on the walls, reflecting the lights, throwing them back into her eyes. She blinked. The clusters of tiny lamps were held by alabaster angels, high on the walls. Each held their cluster as if they were making an offering; calling her into their space. The stained-glass windows she had noticed from the outside of the building now gleamed, delicate and elaborate, filled with pale blues and shimmering pinks.

In the centre of the hall stood a group of twenty students. Jenna stared at them. They stood at barres, swishing their legs in time to the piano music, their arms open, their heads high and poised, their feet immaculate.

Jenna's eyes stung with tears. She recognised two of the dancers. They had auditioned with her all those months ago . . .

An office door opened.

The Head of Dance said, "Jenna Pascoe?"

Jenna turned, frantically trying to hide her tears.

A firm handshake and a pair of smiling eyes greeted her. "I'm delighted to see you again . . . Come in and take a seat."

The door to the office closed. The light blue eyes looked squarely at Jenna.

"Please. Take your time."

Jenna spilled out the story of the darkest summer she had ever spent.

The Head of Dance listened, never interrupting, letting Jenna reach the end.

"And what I've come to ask," Jenna said, her mouth dry, her throat sore, her eyes stinging with hope, "is this. Will you . . . is there still room for me? Next term. In January, could I take up my place?"

The Head of Dance frowned. She slid her glasses over her nose, rummaged for a file, flicked it open. "I remember your audition clearly . . . We wanted you to come very much, it was a unanimous decision . . . But after you wrote to me, I offered your place to someone else."

I knew it . . . I'm too late . . . It's hopeless . . . I'll have to go straight home . . .

"However . . . another student, Monique, she broke her ankle last month. Her parents asked her to go home to Paris. And she's decided not to return."

Jenna's heart leapt. "Does that mean —"

"We *do* make exceptions, Jenna. We're all human, we all have lives beyond the Urdang in which tragic things can happen." She took off her glasses. "You've had a terrible time, but you seem to have come through it remarkably well." She took Jenna's hands in hers. "You'll have missed a whole term, a crucially important one which sets the goals for so much else. You'll need to work really hard to catch up. Are you prepared for that?"

"Yes, oh, yes, of course . . . I'll do everything and more."

"We assess the progress of our students at the end of every term. If you're not up to standard at the end of *next* term —"

"I will be, I promise."

"It's going to be tough, I'll make no bones about it. This will be the only time I can ever make you an exception."

"I understand."

"And between now and the beginning of January, I want you to dance and sing as much as you can . . . Serious, hard, steady, sensible work. Go back to your teachers in Cornwall. Pick up where you left off."

"I will." Jenna's voice shook with joy. "Does that mean you'll —"

"Yes, Jenna." The Head of Dance sat back in her chair and smiled. "I'm delighted to tell you . . . It looks as if we will!"

Jenna stood outside the Urdang and took a deep breath. Her legs shook with relief and excitement.

I did it! I dared to ask . . . Nothing venture, nothing gained. Isn't that what they say?

Drab London looked suddenly transformed. People laughed and teased each other as they jostled past. Couples hugged on corners. Shop windows glittered with Christmas offerings. Frosted gold and silver stars hung over the pavements, caught the breeze and fanned the twilight air.

Resisting the temptation to skip along the street, Jenna hailed a cab.

Aunt Tamsyn is going to get the biggest surprise of her life.

*

"Did you have a good time?" Dad collapsed over a cup of tea at the kitchen table. "Hester and I have been rushed off our feet . . . So, tell me all about it. What did you get up to?"

"It was great."

"And how's that sister of mine?"

"She's great too."

"And?" Dad frowned at her. "Come *on,* Jenna. Talk to me . . . Spill the beans."

Jenna said slowly, "There are a lot to spill."

Dad crashed his cup on to the saucer. "Ah . . . I see . . . That sparkle in your eyes. It means more than just 'I had a lovely time.' "

"Yes, Dad. Can you guess?"

"Oh, Jenn. I think I probably can."

"I'm going to dance again . . . The Urdang have said they'll take me on. I've missed a term, but better late than . . . I've tried so hard to give it up. But I can't."

Dad said quietly, "I never asked you to."

Jenna gaped. "I thought you'd be furious . . . I thought you'd want me here."

"I do . . . I did . . . Only because I was trying to respect your decision."

"But —"

"My dearest Jenna, I've done everything I possibly could to encourage you . . . Paid for your lessons, built you your own studio, fought cat and dog with Mum over it." His eyes behind his glasses were bright with tears. "That day when they accepted you. What did I promise? That nothing in the world could stop you now?"

"Yes, Dad." Jenna eyes burned. "But that was before —"

"*That* was before . . . And *this* is afterwards." He held out his arms. "Now, are you going to give your plumpish, frumpish old dad a hug or what?"

Jenna stood at the doorway to Lelant's village hall. Inside she could hear the thunder of the CD music, Leah's firm voice giving instructions above it.

"*Use* the space. Take the risk. If you don't, you'll never know whether you can be an exciting dancer."

She grinned to herself and pushed at the door.

Leah stopped dead in her tracks. "One moment, please, girls. We have a visitor." She dived towards the CD player and turned it off. She held out her hands to Jenna, her eyes blazing with delight. "I can't believe it . . . Are you a ghost?"

Jenna laughed. "Pinch me and see."

"Have you come to dance?"

"Yes, please. Will you have me back?"

"So you've come to your senses at last . . . Does this mean what I hope it means?"

"It sure does," Jenna said. "Now, can I go and get changed?"

"I haven't sung a single note since Benjie . . . since he —"

Helen sat down at the piano. She looked up at Jenna, her eyes beneath her wild grey fringe bright and understanding. "You haven't exactly had much to sing about."

"No. It was like I kept saying to myself, 'Shut up. Pay the price. Forget who you really are. Get your head down and stay that way.' "

"And now?"

"Now I feel a hundred years older, as if along the way I've forgotten how to be a teenager. But I've remembered who I am." Jenna swallowed. "Could you help me find my singing voice again?"

Helen ran her hands over the keyboard.

Jenna began to sing.

As the notes flooded out of her body, out of her throat,

she felt them change from a shout of hurt and pain into a song of renewal and of joy.

Christmas seemed to pass in a dream. After the holidays were over, Dad started asking around in the Cockleshell for new staff.

"I don't need to advertise," he said. "I know plenty of people who'd love to work here. I want two or three helpers, so I get a chance to see which one I work with best."

"What about Hester?"

"She doesn't want to come back full-time." Dad blushed. "I couldn't have a better friend . . . Friendships at my age are hard to come by. I don't want to spoil it." He stared sadly out of the window at the Digey as the winter streets darkened into night. "Anyway, my Lydia may still come back to me." He turned to Jenna. "I can't stop hoping, you know."

"I'll see her in London," Jenna said. "It'll be difficult, but I promise you we'll meet. We'll *try* to become friends." She looked across at him. "Then I can let you know how she is."

Dad's face brightened. "If she ever needs anything, if she ever wants to see me —"

"Oh, Dad." Impatience and anger and pity washed through her. "If Mum ever wants you, she knows where you are."

"I'm trying not to think about being away from you," Jenna said.

She and Meryn were spending her last evening together at his cottage.

"I just keep on telling myself I'll be back in the holidays."

"You may be back, but you'll be different. You'll be the Urdang's student: devoted, dedicated, disciplined."

Jenna laughed. "That makes me sound very stern and professional."

"But you *will* be. It's a tough life."

Jenna looked up at him. "The tougher the better. The harder the challenge, the higher I shall jump. The more work I have, the less time there'll be to brood about how much I'm missing you."

"Will you phone me every week?"

"You know I will . . . Now, stop all this serious talk before I burst into tears and change my mind."

"Don't do that. I want this evening to be extra special." He stroked her hair. "By the time Easter comes, we'll both

have changed. We may never be together in the same way
again."

"You'll meet someone else." Jenna stared into the fire,
jealousy flicking at her heart. "Someone from St Ives
who'll be happy to stay here, who won't go dashing off to
chase her wild dreams."

"And you," Meryn said teasingly, "you'll meet a dancer
who'll sweep you off your feet. Literally!"

"But the person who made me come to life again is you,
Meryn." Jenna blinked away the tears. "For that I love you
– and I always will."

On the station platform at St Erth, Dad took her in his
arms.

"I'm so proud of you. I know what a fight you've had."

"Take care of yourself, Dad. Promise me."

"Be sure to get plenty of sleep. The first two weeks will
be the worst. You won't know what's hit you."

"And look after Dusty for me. I searched for him
everywhere this morning. He probably didn't want to say
goodbye."

"Tell that sister of mine she's very lucky to have you!"

"I'll be back for Easter. The time will fly."

"Yes." Dad released her. "Go on, then . . ."

"Love you, Dad."

"Quick . . . Start the clock ticking . . . Get on that blooming train."

In the room that would be her home for the next three years, Jenna unpacked her possessions. Clothes in the cupboard. Dance gear in the chest of drawers. Books on the shelf. Files in the desk.

On her bedside table she propped two photographs.

Dad and Benjie, laughing together on Porthgwidden Beach, sitting at one of the picnic tables on a Sunday afternoon, the wind flicking through their hair, Dad's arm round Benjie's shoulder.

Meryn, lean and bronzed in his grey-and-white tracksuit, standing outside the harbour cottage, his dark eyes smiling.

Next to them she placed something she had taken from Benjie's room: the engine from his train set, graceful, solid, bottle-green.

At the Academy, their ballet teacher checked every name and face.

She said, "I'd like to extend a special welcome to our new student, Jenna Pascoe."

Jenna blushed.

"Jenna was unable to join us last term. She knows she'll have to work extra hard to catch up . . . I'm sure you'll all help her and make her feel at home."

The students murmured their welcome.

The teacher's eyes scanned their bodies, picking up on every detail of how they stood, their poise, the eagerness in their eyes, their readiness.

"I hope you've all been exercising in the holidays . . . We can never afford to take time off . . . If we do, our bodies will complain and our work will suffer.

"Right . . . into the centre with you and down on to the floor . . .

"Fine . . . Spread out, use the space in the corners, there's plenty of room . . .

"Piano, please . . . Thank you, Nick . . .

"Are you ready, Jenna?"

"Yes," Jenna said firmly. "I'm ready."

"Right, everyone . . .

"Shall we begin?"